I Goes Shopping

TO JIAN

A Jenny Turnbull Mystery

Jessica Burton

BEST WISHES
JESSICA

RENDEZVOUS PRESS

Text © 2002 Jessica Burton

All rights reserved. No part of this publication may be reproduced, stored in a retrieval system or transmitted, in any form or by any means, electronic, mechanical, photocopying, recording or otherwise, without the prior consent of the publisher.

Cover art by Christopher Chuckry   www.chuckry.com

LE CONSEIL DES ARTS | THE CANADA COUNCIL
DU CANADA | FOR THE ARTS
DEPUIS 1957 | SINCE 1957

We gratefully acknowledge the support of the Canada Council for the Arts for our publishing program.

Napoleon Publishing/RendezVous Press
Toronto, Ontario, Canada
www.rendezvouspress.com

Printed in Canada

05 04 03 02   5 4 3 2 1

National Library of Canada Cataloguing in Publication

Burton, Jessica—
   Death Goes Shopping / Jessica Burton

"A Jenny Turnbull mystery".
ISBN 0-929141-95-4

I. Title.

PS8553.U696243D42 2002   C813'.6   C2002-902961-9
PR9199.4.B87S42 2002

*For my mother
Marion McFarlane Burton*

Acknowledgements

Heartfelt thanks are owed to Roger, Helen, Debbie, Keith, Jackie, Susan, Big Red and all the kids for always believing…

…and also to Bruce and Kal Pattison, Betts and Herbert Engell and Susan Williamson for their unconditional support and encouragement, to Margaret Hart and Joe Kertes of the Humber School for Writers for their best efforts and for never giving up and…

…a special thank you to Eric Wright for cheering me on despite the commas and another one to Jen for her spaghetti sauce.

I am also indebted to my publisher Sylvia McConnell and the Notorious Crime Family for gathering me up with open arms and to editor Allister Thompson for his patient work in bettering my manuscript.

One

When the shoe hit my desk, I was head down and counting elves, so I just reached out and tried to sweep it off.

As promotion director for a large shopping centre, odd items turn up in my office all the time, so unless they're immediately needed, I don't pay much attention. Right now I needed an elf, not a big black shoe.

The shoe didn't budge.

It didn't budge because it landed complete with a foot.

I looked up and saw the foot was at the end of a leg which its owner had lifted onto my desk. He was a huge man whose dark gray suit, white shirt and Paisley tie were topped with two chins and a scowling face. Hands splayed on the wall behind him, he was trying to balance on his one operating leg. Dark eyes, narrowed behind a pair of gold-rimmed bifocals, looked me over carefully and locked on my face.

"Is there something I can do for you?" I hit the phone intercom button that was linked to mall Security. "The administration office isn't really open on Saturdays, you know."

No answer.

I repeated my question and hit the intercom again. I could see this guy was really agitated, and I was alone. In a shopping centre this big, you get all kinds, and it pays to be cautious.

Rosewood Centre is a two-level building shaped like a straightened Z. The main entrance doors, in the middle of the mall, face east. The top and bottom of the zee are major department stores, both with two floors and, of course, their own outside doors as well as entrances onto the mall area. They're connected by a main concourse lined on both sides with ancillary stores, banks and service outlets. Our mall management offices are at the end of a back hallway on the shopping centre's upper level. They're deliberately hard to find in order to discourage drop-in visits from both tenants and customers. Seems the plan wasn't working today.

"I've been looking for you," he said.

He wobbled about a bit, gave up and half-fell, half-sat in the chair on the other side of the desk. His foot stayed where it was.

If I hadn't been so distracted because of the screw-up in my pumpkin delivery, I'd have remembered to lock the outer door. The administration suite has four interior offices and a small kitchen linked by a short hall leading from the fair-sized reception area. My office is on the left as you come in the outer door and turn down the hall. But I hadn't locked the door, and now here I was, facing God knows what, with his shoe on my desk.

"You are the Customer Complaints woman, I take it?" His voice was tight and precise, like his face. "I was told downstairs you'd be up here."

"I'm Jenny Turnbull, the Promotion Director. But I also handle any concerns that customers may have about Rosewood City Centre," I said. "If I can ask again, who are you, and why is your foot on my desk?"

"God give me strength." He looked at the ceiling. "Another bloody Scot."

I felt around under the kneehole opening in the desk with my foot, trying to find my knitting bag and nudge it to where

I could grab a knitting needle in a hurry.

"I'm a customer, that's who. I'm the man who pays your wages, that's who. And I'm the reason you've got a job, that's who."

He tried emphasizing his words by stabbing a finger on the desk but kept missing, because his outstretched leg and a fair-sized paunch kept him from leaning forward. He used the arm of the chair instead. His face was red with effort, but he was determined. That shoe wasn't coming off the desk until he'd had his say.

"I'm Dick…"

Well, that fits, I thought. But if he says Tracy, I'm going for the needle.

"…Simmons, and you just bet, Miss, that I have a concern." His voice lost some of its control. It's pretty hard to be precise with one leg stuck up higher than your belly. "As a matter of fact, it's more than a concern, it's a goddam complaint. And a goddam justified complaint at that."

I raised my eyebrows. He inched his backside forward. The shoe slid closer. The only thing missing was a drum roll.

"Look at that shoe. Just look at it. Now, I ask you."

I looked. Black and highly polished with the number twelve stamped on the sole, it looked about right to me.

"Just what are you asking me, Dick? What am I looking for?"

"Well, any fool could see that," he said. "Look at the repair. Or what's supposed to be a bloody repair. Two hundred dollar Italian shoes ruined. Ruined." He shook his head. "My wife took them in for new soles, and that asshole countryman of yours in that fancy-dancy shoe repair downstairs ruined them. Stupid sonofabitch."

His precision was totally gone now. He sucked in a huge

mouthful of air and slid forward a bit more. His tie slid off to one side, showing a few black hairs in the gap where the fronts of his shirt pulled between the buttons.

"And what's more, when I took the fucking shoes back, the bastard threw me out. Said there was nothing wrong with them. Now, you own this poor excuse of a mall, and I'm asking you, what're you going to do about it?"

Stab, stab went the finger. My father used to do that when I was a kid. I hated it then, and I still hate it. I have a finger too. One that I desperately wanted to show this guy. Whoever said "the clothes bespeak the man" had certainly never met Mr. Simmons. Maybe Mrs. Simmons dressed him.

However, public relations and maintaining a good mall image being important parts of my job, I had to at least be pleasant to this particular Dick, who'd just promoted me. I'd gone straight from working for him to shopping centre owner.

"Besides, he's got no right to throw me out. This is public property. I know my rights. He can't…"

I held up both hands to stop the flow. It worked, but who knew for how long? I'd better make this good, and I'd better make it fast.

"First of all, Mr. Simmons, let me say that I regret that you're upset. I regret it more than you know.

"We want our customers to enjoy their shopping at Rosewood City Centre. And, although we're the only major shopping mall in this area, we never take things for granted. Our policy is to ensure a pleasant, climate-controlled environment to serve the public, and we take whatever measures necessary to implement that policy. Let me tell you just a few of them."

I was on a roll now. Time to trot out the three Bs. Bullshit Baffles Brains.

"We have a $1.2 million annual budget devoted solely to

advertising and promoting the centre, its 214 retail merchants, restaurants and service businesses. That's a dollar per square foot, Mr. Simmons. A healthy sum. There is an administrative staff of five people, including myself; two on-site stationary engineers; a daily maintenance staff plus a night cleaning crew. In addition, the shopping centre has a full complement of security officers headed by an ex-policewoman."

He opened his mouth to start again, but I kept going.

"We also have an Information Booth on the lower level, staffed by three fully-trained people to help you find your way around the building and answer any inquiries you may have. I'm sure you went to there to find out where I could be located."

And just wait till I get down there, I added to myself.

"All of this, Mr. Simmons, to make sure you are a satisfied customer. Apparently, today at least, you're not."

"Damned right, I'm not. And, anyway, I don't give a monkey's fart about any of that." He was shouting now, and his stabbing finger changed to a pointer aimed directly at my face.

My foot was moving faster and faster. Where the hell was that knitting bag? And why wasn't Security answering?

"And I don't want any of this business of you goddam Scots sticking together. Just get my shoes fixed properly or get my money back."

He stopped for a breath. My turn.

"Here's what I propose to do to correct the situation, Mr. Simmons. While being fair to both sides, of course."

I put my hands down and picked up a pencil and scratchpad.

"There's only one way to correct it," he mimicked my accent. "Get my fucking shoes fixed and fixed now, or I'll fix your whole rotten shopping centre.

"In fact, maybe I'll do that, anyway. And let me tell you, Ms. Jenny Bloody Turnbull, Promotion Director, you won't like it. You won't like it one fuckin' bit, and neither will your friend downstairs or your 214 retail merchants, et cetera, et cetera, et cetera."

I dropped the pencil and paper, stood up and leaned towards him, both hands on the desk. I'd had it. First the pumpkins, then the missing elf and now this bottom feeder, and it wasn't even noon yet. This guy needed an attitude adjustment—big time.

"Mr. Simmons," I said. "First, stop swearing. Second, remove your foot. If you don't do these two things, this conversation is over. You'll be escorted from the mall, and I'll issue a ban in your name. One copy will be delivered to the local precinct, which they will lodge in their files, and one copy will be sent to you. Registered mail, of course. What that means, Mr. Simmons, is that you will not be allowed back on this property, which by the way is private, not public, for a period of time which I can and will stipulate. In addition, where do you think your complaint will be filed?"

He took his foot off the desk and straightened in the chair, but I could see we weren't finished. He was furious. His lips had disappeared, and his cheeks were scarlet. But at least my desk was clear and his finger was still. Two points for me and none for him.

I remained standing. I liked looking down at him. "Even if I wanted to, I can't do anything about your complaint right now. Today is Halloween, and the mall is filled with kids and parents, all taking part in our pumpkin-carving, colouring and costume contests. I am not only overseeing the promotion, but have to judge the contests shortly, along with the Mayor and other local dignitaries and press people who were kind enough to give up their Saturday afternoon. I have no intention of cancelling any of that over a pair of shoes.

"Drop them off at the Information Booth on Monday. I'll have several of the shoe store owners examine them, give me their assessment of the repair, and we'll go from there. That's the best I can do and now, I'd like you to leave."

He stood up. "Even if I agree to that—and I haven't yet, mind you—what about that Scotty bastard throwing me out which, by the way, I notice you ignored. What're you going to do about that?"

"Nothing, Mr. Simmons. He's the tenant. He pays the rent and has the right to control the access to that store. What happened is unfortunate, of course, but I really can't do anything about it."

One point for Gord at Star Shoe Repair. And still none for Dick.

I moved around the desk and gestured to the door. He fired one last shot. "Well, I can fucking well do something about it. He won't do that to me in a hurry and get away with it."

He shoved the chair against the wall with a bang and stamped off up the hall. Oh well, as my mother always said, stubborn is as stubborn does. He'd probably calm down over the weekend.

The word "asshole" came back as the outer door closed with a bang. I didn't know whether he meant me or Gord, but who cared? He was gone. I gave it a few seconds then moved quickly up the hall to lock the door.

The reception area houses Shirley, our secretary, all her paraphernalia, and a couch flagged by the standard end tables, lamps and coffee table. A few pieces of no-name art dot the walls.

Turning around, I looked at the couch. Five minutes couldn't hurt. I sank into it with a sigh of relief, kicked off my shoes and put my feet up on the coffee table, trying to organize my thoughts.

Halloween was well under way, even if it'd had a rocky start. Another six hours or so and we could start the clean up, then file the whole event under "D" for "Done". Christmas was next, and it was well in hand, as were the Boxing Day Bonanza and the usual January Sidewalk Sale.

We never did much from my office for Valentine's, so I had a month or so to prepare for our Annual General Meeting in February. The tenants all pay so much per square foot for advertising and promos according to their lease, and the mall owners kick in a dollar amount as well. The tally becomes my promotion budget, and it looked like I was going to have to go for an increase next year. That meant planning a promotion schedule and working out the budget to include increased costs and to justify asking for more money. I'd already made a start on it, so things were in pretty good shape.

The phone on Shirley's desk rang.

"Jenny, it's Mary, down at the Info booth. You're needed at the pumpkin carving area. There's three eight-foot white rabbits dancing to rap music. And they've got all the kids doing it, too. The stores are complaining."

I knew exactly what was going on. "Mary, just get one of the Security guys to walk over there and have a word with the DJ. Tell him to cool it, turn down the music and tell kids' stories or something. That'll stop the rabbits. I don't mind the dancing, but those kids are working with knives down there. I wouldn't want any of them getting carried away to the beat."

Halloween. I hate it. It falls right behind Christmas and just before my hair on a list of things to hate that's stuck to the wall beside my desk. An ex-boyfriend, staring at my head, once told me that red hair was caused by a recessive gene. He probably made it up because we were in a shouting match at the time, but though he's long gone, the remark still rankles.

Most of the time, I love my job. It's usually exciting and very often frustrating, but it's never boring, and that's enough to keep me at it.

October 31st, though, always falls into the latter category. Trying to organize a couple of hundred midget witches, ghosts and goblins, some with crayons for colouring, some with knives for carving and some just with knives, is an exercise in frustration. Most of the little kids arrive with parents. They're not the problem. Actually, I enjoy watching them get a kick out of the different activities. It's the older ones who want a chance to hack at anything with their blades, including each other, that I can do without.

Our mall Security crew hates Halloween, the maintenance staff won't talk to me for at least two days before it because they know what the clean-up's going to be like and the rest of the management team makes sure they're never on duty that day.

So why do we do it? The community expects it as a special children's event, and God forbid we should alienate the customers' kids. The local rag even gives us free coverage, and that's next to impossible to get, so here we are. This was my third Halloween promotion, and I wasn't having a good time so far.

I'd arrived at the mall about seven that morning, because shopping centre promotions are governed by Murphy's Law, and I like to buy a little extra time.

The four high school kids I'd hired that week to help out were waiting at the front entrance. So was a mile-high pile of pumpkins.

"What the hell are these doing here? They're supposed to be inside. I had a maintenance guy scheduled to open the promotion doors round the back at six this morning so the truck could drive right in and park next to the stage."

The tallest kid, Joshua, shrugged his shoulders and spread

his hands. The other three formed a line behind him, rally caps on tight. Backup, I guess. This sure wasn't going to be their fault.

"We just got here, and they were here already. Guess the driver went to the wrong door. He was just leaving 'cause he tried ringing the night bell but nobody showed and he knew you needed them for today and, anyway…he wasn't taking them back so he unloaded the truck and said that would cost you extra on the bill…'cause of he wasn't supposed to unload the truck…'cause of he's got a bad back and you gotta hope it doesn't get worse 'cause of this…and Joe here tried to get security to let us in, but they wouldn't…'cause of they don't know us so we couldn't do anything anyway…so we just waited for you."

Having got rid of all that, he stepped back with the others and the four of them looked at me, arms folded across their chests. They suspected what was coming, and I didn't disappoint them. "You guys'll have to take them in."

I got out my keys, opened the small door to the left of the main entrance and shooed them inside.

"Joe, go to the promo storage area. The one at the back of the Food Court behind Tijuana Taco, not the upstairs one where you got the stage and stuff yesterday. Look for the door that says Promotion Department." I handed him the key. "You'll find a flat dolly and a couple of shopping carts. Take Vijay and Roger with you and don't dawdle. It's half past seven already."

Joe and his buddies veered off to the left, moving fast. It was like watching one body with six legs. No need to tell teenagers where a shopping centre Food Court is.

Joshua and I went to the stage outside one of the mall's two department stores. The day before, the boys had set it up beside eight six-foot tables placed in a hollow square. The tables, where the kids would do the carving, were covered with newsprint cut from end rolls, courtesy of our local paper. The stage held four rows of chairs for parents and later, the judges, and a sound system was in place for the emcee—a local DJ-come-entertainer, who was being paid handsomely to keep the kids happy and, please God, reasonably under control.

"First off, Josh, we can't block the entrance to the department store. Those pumpkins are going to take up more room loose than they would've on the truck."

He loped back and forth in his Nikes, striding around the stage and tables. "Why don't we pile them up in the middle of the square and they can help themselves?" he asked. "We got all that empty space."

"Because some kid'll pull one from the bottom and start an avalanche. No, I think a better idea is to put as many on the ground here as you can." I paced off a floor space about fifteen feet square. "No more than two, maybe three deep. Leave the others in the back hallway over there through the maintenance doors. You're scheduled to be here anyway, giving them out, so Roger and Vijay can stay with you and go back and forth for more as you need them."

"What about the costume parade and the colouring contest? Aren't a couple of us supposed to help with them?"

"I'll manage those," I said. "There's never much to do once they're started, and they're pretty easy. Practically run themselves. Joe can help me see to the parade. It's only going from one end of the mall to the other, and it doesn't start till this afternoon.

"While you guys handle the pumpkins, he can pass out crayons and paper for the colouring contest in the Food Court. We lined up some of the tables last night for the kids to use. And, unless their parents dump the little angels for free babysitting, they can keep an eye on their own kids. We just have to make sure the colouring is finished in time for Maintenance to clear up for the lunch crowd."

I mentally dusted off my hands. Now for the sneaky part. "I want all four of you up in my office the minute you finish here. Your costumes were delivered yesterday."

"Costumes?" His voice went up four octaves. "What costumes?"

"Oh, did I forget to tell you? My helpers always wear costumes for promotions. Makes them easier to spot if they're needed, and the little kids like 'em too. I'm sure I mentioned it when we talked about this job probably being a long-term thing for you guys. Don't forget, upstairs, the minute you're finished."

God, that was below the belt, but hey, I'm for whatever works. "While I'm at it, I'll write out ID cards for the four of you so Security'll know you next time."

An hour later, four large, white rabbits were at their stations, ready for the onslaught.

Now, listening to Mary on the phone, I realized my mistake was telling Joshua to take charge of getting the DJ set up. I'd even told him to help pick the music.

"Mary, I'm going down to check out how the colouring contest is going. If anyone needs me, I'll be the one in the Food Court with no crayon."

"One more thing, Jenny, before you hang up," Mary said. "Susan took a call for you earlier. A Mr. Doug White. Said he was supposed to be Santa but has to cancel. Said sorry, but he just can't do it. Something about being too nervous, and he doesn't want you to call him back."

"What?" I held the phone away from my ear and shook it, hoping her words would fall out and evaporate. "What did you say?"

"Susan took a call…"

"Mary, I heard you the first time. I was just wishing I hadn't. I didn't mean to yell at you. Don't worry about it. It's just one more thing for the list."

I sat back down on the couch, staring blankly at the carpet. Dick Simmons and the rappin' rabbits were nothing compared to this. This was Murphy's Law at its finest.

Other than "collect the rent", there are very few credos in the shopping centre industry, but there is one for promotion directors that means your job if you ignore it: "If you can't do Christmas right, don't do it at all."

That's it. Plain and simple. It doesn't matter what else you do all year, if you muff the Christmas promo, you're gone.

The mall's annual Santa Claus Parade was scheduled, as usual, for the second weekend in November. With the exception of miscounting the elves, I had everything in place. The majorettes, the Police Pipe Band, all booked, extra security was lined up for crowd control, the radio and print advertising was booked, a new jingle written and the signage was just about finished. The Christmas decorations had been cleaned and touched up, all the light bulbs checked and Santa's sleigh had been repainted, as it was every year.

I had cartons of candy canes in the storage rooms ready for his sack, and the whole "Have Your Picture Taken With Santa" setup was ready to go. Last year we'd taken seventeen thousand pictures over six weeks. It was a huge headache to set up and control, what with staffing, inventory and the bookkeeping that came with it, so this year I'd contracted it out. The company I'd hired provided camera, staff, film, everything. All I had to do was put Santa in the chair and take my share of the money. A snap.

Sixty-five per cent of our whole year's retail business is done during the Christmas season, and the restaurants and other outlets also depend on the increase in customers during those six weeks.

Christmas is the one time of year when people happily give up regular shopping habits and drive longer distances to get what they want. And very often, the biggest magnet is what kind of Santa setup is in the mall. Ours is the most popular for miles around, and we're at the intersection of two major highways, so we're easy to get to. Our shopper count at Christmas is in the neighbourhood of three hundred thousand people a week, all with money and all prepared to spend it.

But right now, Saturday, October 31, two weeks and counting, a disaster was in the making. I'd lost Santa.

Two weeks before the parade, and the old geezer had up and quit before he'd even started. Shame he hadn't thought about nervousness in August when I'd hired him. I'd been so pleased to get him, too. He certainly had the build for it. An egg with legs. He wouldn't even have needed the belly padding.

Next Thursday was our monthly board meeting of the Merchants Association, and my presentation of the centre's Christmas arrangements would be first on the agenda. I had five days to find a replacement Santa. There was nothing, absolutely nothing on God's green earth, that would make me enter that meeting without one.

Now, Jenny, I thought. Calm down. You can do this. Put Halloween to rest first. Panic about Santa on Monday.

I checked the wall clock. Almost quarter to twelve. The Mayor and his entourage weren't due until later in the afternoon, and the trick or treaters were probably tied up with fries and a pop. There was time to sneak a quick burger.

I'd double-promised Helen I'd start eating healthy food

today, but that was before Dick Simmons, Halloween and Santa. She'd understand, I reasoned.

Helen Lemieux has been the mall Security Chief for four years, ever since the centre opened, and we share an old house together. Both in our early thirties, we'd become instant friends when I'd joined the management team a couple of years ago. Two days into the job, we'd gone for lunch together, and two minutes into the meal, I was telling her my life story—particularly as it related to the guy I was involved with at the time. A guy who'd just told me, the night before, he thought we should move in together, but I should understand he believed in "open" relationships.

"And you said?" she asked.

"I told him exactly what he could do with his belief."

Sometimes you meet people, and they just fit right into your life. That was us. It was almost as if there was a karma of sorts working in our favour. I suspect something in my Scottish ancestry reacts to her Cree heritage. Maybe we're psychic sisters, I don't know, but we do have the ability to sometimes finish each other's sentences, and one of us will very often know exactly what the other is thinking. It doesn't bother us, we enjoy it, but a lot of the time it spooks other people.

Helen's into healthy eating and alternative medicine. She exercises relentlessly and spends a lot of time researching nutrition and collecting heart-smart cookbooks.

I'm into eating—period, any medicine that works and my favorite exercises are reading and knitting. The only thing I've managed to collect is a '56 Chevy. She's working on changing all that and, with the exception of the car, I've promised to try.

I got up to go just as the two-way radio on Shirley's credenza crackled, and Helen's voice came on calling my name.

God, I thought. Caught already.

"Jenny, pick up the radio." Her voice was urgent. "Jenny, pick it up. Emergency."

"It was only gonna be a burger, Helen," I said. "No fries. Honest."

"Never mind that," she said. "You'll eat later. Get down here fast, Jenny. I'm in the Food Court. There's been a shooting."

Two

I heard the noise first. Pealing out like a summons. Demanding attention.

Please God, not the kids. Don't let it be the kids, I prayed as I got off the escalator on the ground floor and ran towards the Food Court, a sunken area in the middle of the ground floor which backs onto the west wall. It boasts the usual mixture of fast food outlets and a common eating area furnished with little square pedestal tables, each with four stools.

Rounding the corner by the Juice Nook, I plowed into a sea of bodies, some running towards me, others, like me, heading on the run to the Food Court, shouting at the top of their lungs, despair and pleading evident in every voice.

"Cindy…Mommy's coming, Cindy."

"Paul, where are you Paul? Can you hear me?"

"Dear God, I can't see him. Jim, why can't I see him?"

"Billy…"

"Katy…I can't find Katy."

The terrible litany came from all sides. Flashing lights from emergency vehicles outside added an eerie backdrop to the voices, pulsating, keeping time. I could see a group of police officers and firemen trying to clear a path for four, maybe five paramedics pulling stretchers, and, up above the whole thing, hung the fifty-foot banner I'd had made up for the promotion. The eighteen inch letters spelled out "Happy Halloween", and they too were lit intermittently by red and yellow flashes.

Peter, one of Helen's uniformed security people, was just up ahead where the main aisle of the mall opened onto the seating area. He was desperately trying to halt the rush. Parents were grabbing at him, clawing at his arms and shouting kids' names.

"Please, people, stay back. You must stay back now. Keep this space clear."

He saw me and motioned me over.

"God, Peter, what's happened?" Heart pounding, I clutched his sleeve. Panic spread through me. I felt like I was underwater and couldn't push my way to the surface.

"Jenny, there's been a shooting. Three people. Two dead and one nearly. Helen needs you to sort out the kids. She's over by the pizza place," He handed me a walkie-talkie. "Said to give you this. Keep it on and keep it close."

There was another surge forward as more people came around the corner. Over his shoulder, I could see stores on the other side of the mall closing and locking their doors.

"Peter, you'll never stop these people." I took a couple of deep breaths, trying to stop shaking and regain some self-control. "They need to get to their kids. We'll have a better chance of helping from inside the food area." Though, God knows, it was the last place I wanted to be.

"Please, sir, ma'am, please." He gave it one last try, peeling a woman's fingers off his sleeve. She held a baby tightly to her breast with the other hand, and her face was ashen, lined with streaks of mascara. "This area has to be cleared. Stay back now. Everything's under control."

Knowing it wasn't, they ignored him and kept pushing forward, scattering into the Food Court, heading for the back wall and their children.

"I think you're right, Jenny. I'm useless here." He put his arm around me and gave me a quick, steadying squeeze. "Let's go."

We pushed our way through the crowd across the courtyard to Paul's Pizza.

It was a bizarre scene, like the final act in an avant garde play. The food outlet's counter was hidden by a phalanx of cops, a solid wall of blue. In front of them, Helen stood facing a semi-circle of people. She was flanked by three of her Security staff and a huge white rabbit. Their arms were joined to form a solid line, trying to keep some distance between themselves and the couple of dozen people straining to see what lay behind the cops.

Off to the right, two or three small groups of people were hemmed in by more police who had their notebooks out, and a couple of officers were unreeling yellow tape, one end of which was tied to a sign stand, advertising pizza by the slice. Still more were herding people to the back of the Food Court, trying to control a panicky crowd of frightened kids and distraught parents.

Helen looked over the heads of the onlookers and spotted us. She freed one of her hands and gestured in the air with her radio. I put mine to my ear.

"Jenny, do you have something I can cordon off this area with?"

"Send the rabbit over." My fingers were trembling so hard I couldn't get the transmit button to work. I didn't want to go over there, to get any closer. I tried the button again. "Send Joe over."

"Who the hell is Joe?" Her voice was strained. "I don't have a Joe."

"The rabbit, Helen. Send me the fucking rabbit."

I watched as she dropped Joe's paw, raised herself up on her toes and spoke into the mouth of the costume, pointing towards me. A bubble rose in my throat, but I managed to swallow it back down.

"Joe, don't speak." I held up a hand as he came near. "Just lose the outfit right here and get over to the storage at the back of the taco place. Bring the screens we use for the Blood Donor Clinic. All of them. Peter, you'd better go and help. They're pretty awkward to carry."

Joe took off the rabbit head. He was refrigerator white. Poor kid hadn't reckoned on this for his first after-school job.

"But I've just got underwear on."

"Joe, I don't care if you're starkers. This is an emergency. There's no time to shuffle around in that suit and besides, nobody'll pay any attention. Listen, there's an old sweatsuit of mine hanging behind the door in the storage. Put that on. Now move it."

They were back in five minutes, five minutes that seemed to take an hour to tick past. I stood and waited, anchored to the spot by the awful keening sound from the back area. It was mixed with kids' voices now, scared and crying, needing the comfort of the familiar.

I looked at my watch and was amazed to see it was just after twelve. Only about half an hour since Dick Simmons had been in my office. Surely to God, this couldn't be his doing. I shook my head. Not over a pair of shoes. It was too absurd.

"Move aside, please," Peter called. "Move aside."

He held the front of the screens, with Joe bringing up the rear. They carried them like a battering ram and waded into the crowd around Helen. She started directing her staff to put them up and hide what she was guarding. A man at the edge of the crowd stepped backwards into me, and I dropped the radio. I bent over to pick it up and he bumped me again, sending me to my knees.

Just then, the crowd parted, and I saw the carnage.

In a heartbeat, I was centred in silence. I heard no sound, saw no movement. My brain, bereft of logic or thought, saw death and could register only the horror.

Two bodies were slumped across a table.

They lay, one with its head tucked tightly into the other's neck, almost as if they had fallen asleep in a lovers' embrace. The face turned towards me had a couple of red circles on the cheek and above one eye. It was lying on a paper plate holding the remains of a pizza. A second plate poked out from the shoulders of the other body. It, too, had bits of food spilling onto the table.

An arm from each drooped down towards feet that splayed away from the wooden pedestal of the little table and rested, lifeless, on their sides.

It was a macabre mirror image.

Two large soft drink cups lay beside the feet, straws bent. I could see drops of blood from the edge of the table hitting the side of one cup and slowly, so slowly, falling to the floor. They left little splatter marks like a child's spin painting, and the red matched, exactly, the red in the pattern of the sweater on one of the arms.

Just off to the left, I saw another figure lying on its side on the floor. The legs in blue jeans and feet in sneakers weren't moving either, as if their owner had fallen asleep.

Finally, mercifully, my eyes closed.

"C'mon, Jenny," Helen said, her voice calm but tight. "Take a few deep breaths. Come on now, get beyond it."

She knelt beside me, one hand on my shoulder, giving my face sharp little taps with the other.

"In through your nose and out through your mouth," she coached me, "just keep breathing. That's right. You can do this, Jenny. I need you to do this. Come on now."

We got me to my feet after a couple of minutes.

"I'll…"

"…be okay," she finished. Her voice softened a bit. "I know you will, hon. Just keep focussed."

"Helen, that man's got slices of pepperoni on his face. Can't somebody just take them off? He looks so sad with bits of sausage stuck to his face."

"It's not pepperoni, Jenny. They're bullet holes. He's dead. They're both dead."

"But they can't be dead, Helen, there isn't enough blood. Shouldn't there be more blood?"

"Jenny, don't think about that now. You've got a job to do. I need you to concentrate on the kids over there."

"But who is it, Helen? Who are they? I mean, I know who one of them is. I think I do, anyway."

I knew I was babbling, but my mouth just wouldn't stop. "I recognized a sweater, Helen. On an arm. It was hanging down, and I recognized it. Please don't say it's Cathy from the wool store. If it's Cathy from the wool store, Helen, I'm not going to like it. Can she be the one who's just wounded, Helen? Please?"

"Hang it up, Jenny, I don't have time for this." Her tone sharpened. "Here's what I need you to do."

She turned me to face the far end of the Food Court, where the colouring contest had been going on.

"Take your kid, Joe or whatever, and get some semblance of order going over there," she said. "The mall's been closed down. The police are controlling all the exits, and the parking lot's barricaded off. Nobody leaves until they give the okay, and that could easily be five or six hours from now, if not longer."

She gave me a little push.

"If you can get that area organized and settled down a bit, it'll help. Besides," she gave a little grin, "you got them in here, so I guess they're yours. Look at it as your next project."

That was dirty pool, and she knew it. Any time I heard somebody say they were bored or fed up, I'd snap back: "You need a project. You can't be bored if you have a project. I'm never bored, because I always have a project."

She was right, of course. In a bad situation, and this surely was a bad situation, I'm better at doing than talking. I was starting to pace back and forth, nodding my head. It's a habit of mine when I need to regroup and get organized. Helen says I look like an ostrich, but it works for me.

"But Cathy…" I looked at Helen's face and saw it. "It is her, isn't it?"

"Yes, Jenny."

"But…"

"Not now. I've got work to do, and so have you, so let's get to it. I'm going to be tied up with the police, so keep your radio handy. We'll talk that way. Two of my people have gone to the pumpkin carving area to stop the contest. I told them to tell your other three kids to change and come here on the double to help. Talk to you later."

And she was gone.

Poor Joe. I'd forgotten about him. Looking around, I spotted him next to Peter, dressed in a salmon-pink sweatsuit. I went over, grabbed his arm and we pushed-pulled our way through the throng, me issuing instructions as we went.

I cleared off one of the tables, scattering paper and crayons to the floor, and Joe climbed up just as Joshua, Vijay and Roger arrived with the disc jockey in tow.

Joe hooked two fingers in his mouth and let out a loud, piercing whistle. It took a couple of tries, but finally the crowd around us quietened down enough for me to be heard.

"Can I have your attention please? I'm Jenny Turnbull from the mall management office, and these boys are on my staff."

Keep it short, I thought. No need to feed the frenzy.

"The police officers have closed the mall, and it could be a few hours before we can reopen, so our first priority now is to get you together with your children as quickly and calmly as possible."

A man in front of the group stepped forward. There was a woman, his wife probably, hanging on to the bottom of his sweatshirt. "And just exactly how do you plan to do that?"

"The kids'll do it. They know their own parents, so if you just line up along the back wall, the boys'll bring the children to you one at a time."

He took another step forward, chin thrust out. "I'm not lining up anywhere. I'm gonna look for my kid, lady, and I'm gonna look for him now."

After the morning I'd had already, this guy was enough to put the tin lid on my public relations skills. I planted myself in his path.

"Look, buster, we're all having a bad time right now, but I'm not having these children upset any more than they are already. So get back with the other parents or I'll get an officer over here, and he'll put you back."

We stood nose to nose for a few seconds. I kept quiet then, because I knew the next one to speak would lose. Finally, with bad grace and a lot of muttering, back he went and the boys began the pairing process.

I sat down at one of the tables in a spot where I could watch the kids join their mothers and fathers, praying that there would be no leftover parents or little ones, thanking my luck that I had hired those boys. If they never want to wear costumes again, that's okay, I thought.

It took less than fifteen minutes for the families to join up and, wonder of wonders, nobody was left unmatched.

I waved the boys and the DJ over and handed Joshua my keys. "Take Roger and go upstairs to my office. There's four cartons marked 'Seniors Day' in the cupboard at the back. Bring them down.

"Joe, you and Vijay gather all these tables and push them together into three or four long rows with stools on both sides. The cartons the boys are getting are filled with decks of cards, board games like checkers and backgammon and that sort of thing. Spread them on the tables and try to get people started amusing themselves."

"What can I do, Jenny?" asked the DJ. Poor guy looked shaken. He wasn't much older than my boys.

"Maybe you could start a storytelling corner for the little kids, Jim. They're going to be the hardest to contain for any length of time."

On any normal day in a shopping centre, people are like water—they spread out and find their own level. Today, of course, wasn't normal. They weren't allowed to spread out, and their level was getting pretty high, although I could certainly understand why. I can't stand to have my choices taken away either. I saw a small crowd talking to the officer over beside the entrance doors. He was shaking his head and motioning them away.

Feeling like a cat that's just been dragged through a hedge backwards, I crossed my arms on the table and put my head down. I wanted nothing more than a wonderful, deep, lung-sucking drag on a cigarette. If only I hadn't let Helen help me stop smoking. I know it's not healthy. I know it can kill you. I know it makes your clothes stink. In fact, I know all the sensible answers, but by God, it's a wonderful pastime. I looked over at a guy sitting in the smoking area. He'd probably let me have a puff if I asked him. Smokers understand these things.

I straightened up just as the boys came over and dragged a stool each to the table. The rally caps were back on. Joe's looked a little odd with the pink sweatsuit.

"What's next?" asked Vijay. "What'dya want us to do now, Jenny?"

Thank the Good Lord for teenagers. They've got a wonderful way of seeing things in black and white, no grays. Especially these teenagers. In one morning they'd been involved in two murders with a possible third, lugged a couple of hundred pumpkins around, been made to dress as rabbits and been locked in the building, but that was okay, that was history. This was now, so let's get to it.

"Lunch is next," I said. "We can't do much more here and, anyway, I'm hungry."

I've never understood people who say they're too upset to eat. To me, upset needs comfort, and comfort equals food.

I looked around. We were inside a ring of yellow tape and police officers. The only people coming and going through the doors were in uniforms of one kind or another.

"Well, the Food Court's sealed off with us inside, and pizza's definitely out, so I guess it's burgers, souvlaki or Chinese, they're the only ones open." I handed Joe and Roger some money. "Get some of everything."

While the boys lined up for our food, I used the radio to call the Information Booth. We needed the upper management in here for damage control, and we needed them fast. Never mind that the Mayor and his group, complete with the press, would be here any time now, the first giant headache was going to be the reaction from the tenants.

Retailers have their own logic. If sales are good, it's because they're doing something right, but if the numbers are down, it's because mall management is doing something wrong, and somebody gunning down their livelihood sure fit that bill nicely.

I spotted Michael Leung, president of the Merchants Association, standing on the far side of the tape, looking at the scene. The managers of the mall's two department stores were on his left, one of them talking to an officer. None of them were smiling. I slid around to another stool so my back was towards them.

The radio came to life.

"Yes, Jenny?"

"Mary, get on the phone and call Mr. Graham and Keith Armstrong at home. We're going to need them as soon as they can get here." Bob Graham was our mall manager, and Keith was his assistant.

"Helen's already done that, Jenny. They're on their way, and the Mayor and the others have been taken to the empty space round the corner from where you are. The one that used to be the video arcade. The police are using it for interviews and witnesses and stuff. They've taken the chairs and tables from your pumpkin carving to use."

"Thanks, Mary."

Well, as I saw things, that was it for now. The parents and the kids were occupied, Security was dealing with the police, the police were dealing with the Mayor, and Leung and his buddies couldn't get at me. Boy, I love it when things are under control. All I had to do now was eat.

Three

"Okay, Helen, what's the scoop?"

She was over by the stove. "Just let me finish here, and I'll fill you in."

I'd been home since just before eight o'clock, impatient for the latest news and knowing Helen, with her inside lines to the cop shop, would have it. She must have been talking to somebody, because it was midnight now, and she'd only been home about twenty minutes.

George Anderson, the Duty Inspector in charge of the "incident", as it was being called for now, had finally permitted people to leave the mall about seven.

Talk about a long, tiresome day.

The coroner had arrived at the Food Court about one-thirty and declared two of the victims, one male, one female, dead at the scene. The third, a young twenty-something man, had been rushed to hospital earlier, accompanied by a police escort.

I thought, and I'm sure most of the people around me did too, that once the bodies were gone, we'd be allowed to leave.

No such luck.

At three, another team of officers had shown up and started taking pictures of the Food Court. Helen managed to break away and join us for a quick bite. She said the second wave was the Identification Unit, whose job it was to photograph everything in sight, starting with the big picture as it were and going on to specific items. And boy, did they get specific. It took well over two hours for them to finish, then a flat cart was wheeled in and the six large, plastic trash bins that serve the food area were carted off.

"Why're they doing that, Jenny?" Joe asked.

"Gonna search them for the gun, I guess. I can't think of anything else they'd want them for." I pointed over to the door behind the Pizza Place. "I saw three guys going in there while you were getting our lunch, so they're obviously searching along the back halls, too."

While this was going on, everyone in the Food Court was questioned systematically to determine where they were when the shooting occurred. A few people, most likely the ones that were actually eating lunch when the murders happened, were led off, presumably to the witness room, for further questioning.

The atmosphere had become pretty tense by then. Any interest in watching the police and emergency crews do their job began to pall after a while, and restlessness set in.

The only smiling faces belonged to the Food Court tenants. Except for the Pizza place, they'd had a captive audience for lunch, and probably the best dinner hour ever, and I was certain the mall's four sit-down restaurants couldn't be too unhappy either.

Around three-thirty, after showing my business card to an officer and having Helen vouch for me, I was allowed to go back up to the office, escorted of course, to get my knitting. No point in wasting knit one, purl one time, but every few rows I'd stop and look over to where I'd seen Cathy's body. Death was unbelievable, incomprehensible. She and I had become quite friendly over the years during my visits to her wool store for supplies. How could she have been shot? Surely it was a mistake. Finally, I put the knitting back in the bag and just sat, thinking about the even larger implications of the day's events.

Any shooting in any public place is a tragedy that always grabs attention, probably because it underlines our own vulnerability. A seemingly random shooting in a major regional shopping centre was a disaster of immense proportions. The media would have a field day with this. Talk about negative publicity. Three people, not only gunned down, but gunned down in the busiest spot in the mall on the busiest day of the week, at the busiest time of the day. And all they were doing was eating lunch. Stir in the fact that the mall was full of kids at the time, and you've got a story tailormade for six-inch headlines. This would give us more coverage than my total budget for the year could buy.

My mind shrivelled thinking about all the fancy dancing it was going take to offset the ramifications of the events.

The mall's slogan is "Rosewood City Centre—Our Prices Are On Target."

I got a quick mental picture of a cartoon showing one of our print ads. The caption read "But then, so are you."

I got the knitting back out of the bag and started again, going faster this time.

At seven o'clock, the yellow tape came down, and the exodus began.

"Boy, look at them go," said Roger. "Guess they're all sick of this place by now, huh?"

"I've had enough, too," said Joe. "Okay if we leave, Jenny, or do you want to do the clean-up now?"

"Not bloody likely. Let's do it tomorrow," I said. "There's been a management meeting called for nine in the morning, so if you guys can be here by two or so, we'll clean up then. Thanks, guys."

"Bye." They all stood up and were, in a word, gone.

I couldn't find Helen, Bob Graham or Keith, but then I didn't try too hard. The Information Booth staff had closed up and left and besides, I'd had enough. My knees were aching from their drop to the floor, and I'd started to think about Santa again. It was time to go home.

•

Now Helen and I were in the kitchen of my downstairs flat in the old house we shared. It had been the original farmhouse of the area before developers had moved in and built a subdivision around it. Tom, our landlord, had inherited the house from his father who had, in turn, inherited it from his father. Helen and I had subsequently inherited it from Tom—at least as temporary caretakers.

I'd dated Tom in a friendly, casual sort of way, a couple of years back, around the time he'd been finishing his doctorate on ancient languages with a special interest in Egyptology. An offer had come for him to take a five-year appointment in Luxor as a visiting professor, and he'd jumped at the chance, taking Helen and me out to dinner to celebrate.

"The only drawback is the house," he said. "I'm uncomfortable about closing it up for that long, and even if I did close it, I can't afford to fly back and forth checking on it."

"We'll look after it," Helen and I said almost in unison. "We'll rent it. You won't have a care in the world."

"Sweet Lord, you two are scary." Tom dropped his fork. "I thought I'd got used to this talking in stereo, but I guess I haven't."

"But you know," he continued, "that's not a bad idea. My father always felt the house was haunted, though I've sure never seen any sign of it. But, if he was right, then you two are naturals."

And so, after a bit of negotiation, here we are. We haven't seen or heard any uninvited guests or unusual activities, but there does seem to be a particular cold spot in the cupboard under the stairs—a cold spot that comes from nowhere, goes nowhere and does nothing. Occasionally, we take our cups of tea and sit on the floor staring at the cupboard, but we usually only get cold and, since we don't know what we're watching for, we just give up and go on about our business. Sometimes, when Helen's not home, I talk to my mother there.

Thanks to the clever planning of Tom's grandfather, there's a sun porch upstairs for Helen, a verandah downstairs for me, and Tom had converted the mud room off the kitchen into an extra bathroom, so there's no fighting over showers. An old carriage shed out back, for which I thank heaven daily, houses my '56 Chevy, but the house's ultimate decadence is the log-burning fireplace in the kitchen.

We've lived here just over a year now, and one of us is gonna have to marry Tom, because we don't intend to move out. Or maybe we can just slice him off a room.

Helen opted for the three rooms on the upper floor, saying the stairs would be good exercise for her which suits me just fine. I've got the downstairs rooms, and we share the large kitchen, which also suits me just fine. Quite often, when Helen has a day off, she'll take a cooking fit, and I come home to find the table set, a gourmet dinner ready and a bottle of Mountain Chablis on ice.

I'm a good enough cook, but my repertoire runs to dishes like meatloaf and chips, bangers and mash, and I only make a roast beef dinner as an excuse to have Yorkshire pudding.

•

So here I was, sitting in a rocker with my feet propped up on a kitchen chair and my knitting needles clicking along like a freight train. When I was a kid in Scotland, we travelled a lot by train. My sister and I drove our mother crazy chanting "Katy did, Katy didn't. Katy did, Katy didn't" in time to the rhythm of the wheels. Sometimes I find myself doing it now, when I knit.

My left knee had a bag of frozen corn niblets across it, and the label on the designer pouch covering the right one said "Peaches and Cream, Flash Frozen".

Helen looked at my knees. Grinning, she patted the bags.

"Is this some kind of tribal medicine lore handed down through your family, Jenny?"

"For your information, smartass, it's First Aid 101—Ice packs for swelling and bruising. And just so's you know, the Scots had clans, not tribes." I turned the bags over. "These are great because they mould right around my knees."

"Your knobby knees," she said. "I'll never understand why you're so skinny, given the junk you eat. As a matter of fact, looking at your legs now, I think we should tie knots in your nylons for knees."

"Cute, Helen, real cute. Now, let's have it. I've been quivering for hours. If I knit any faster, these needles'll melt. What happened after I left?"

Helen carried a tray to the table and set down two mugs of tomato soup and a plate stacked with grilled cheese sandwiches. A little comfort food for a midnight snack, and a fire going. How could you hate it?

"I don't know if eating cheese at midnight's a good idea, especially nippy old cheddar," she said, handing me a mug and a sandwich. "They say it gives you nightmares, you know."

"Who's they'?" I dipped my sandwich in the soup and swirled it about a bit. "I'm looking around and I don't see any 'they'."

I bit off a chunk and dipped the sandwich again.

"Anyway, my nightmare's already booked, and it's probably going to be the same as yours." I stared at my bit of sandwich. "You know, I can hardly believe Cathy Haggerty is dead. It doesn't seem quite real."

"I know," said Helen. "Just her luck to pick that table. I wonder who was there first, though I don't suppose it matters much."

A shopping centre food area is like the setting for musical chairs. Customers walk around with their tray of food, and the minute they spot a seat, they're in it. Doesn't matter who else is there. It's enough that you found a stool. After all, you're not there to socialize, though some do. The principle is "fast in, fast out."

"She was such a nice person and so helpful." I couldn't let it go. "I was just in her store yesterday to see if the rest of my wool was in yet, this new stuff she put me on to. How can I be talking to her one day, and she's dead the next? She was going to order me a particular shade of green they've just introduced. I really need that colour now I've changed my whole pattern around."

What Helen didn't know was that my current project is a Fair Isle sweater for her as a surprise Christmas present.

Cathy had called me at the beginning of September, excited about finding this new supplier.

"Jenny, you have to come down and look at this wool I've just got in," she'd said. "You won't believe it. Pure wool, beautiful colours, a great price and the best part is they leave eighty per cent of the lanolin in, so it's not itchy. I'm telling you, this one's outstanding."

Well, of course, one look and I was sold. What knitter can resist a brand new product? There's something about all those balls of virgin wool that reaches out to you. It's like looking at the eyes of dogs or cats in the animal shelter-—they all say "take me, take me."

According to Cathy, this knitting yarn was actually produced by a sheep farmer just a two hour drive from here. Apparently, he'd formed some kind of co-op with other farmers who shipped him their wool and he, in turn, baled it, sent it to Allentown, Pennsylvania, to get washed and then on to several different mills to be spun and dyed.

It had all the earmarks of a local success story, and the wool was indeed a quality yarn so, naturally, I bought enough for a sweater and was off and running on a new project—a project that had just suffered a sudden setback.

Oh well, I'll deal with it at the beginning of the week, I thought. If push comes to shove, I can always find the farmer. Getting back to the subject at hand, I took another sandwich.

"And that guy from the florist's, Gerry what's-his-name? I heard he was the other body, the one with the pepperoni. I never liked him much, what with his smarmy winking and gestures every time I walked past the store, but that's no reason to want him dead. God, was he even thirty?"

"Twenty-eight," Helen said. "Gerry Menard. And you weren't the only one who didn't like him much, Jenny. Nobody did, now I come to think of it. He was such a jerk, and I'm convinced he used the florist's job as a front for other things, although I could never come up with something concrete enough to do anything about it."

"Like what?" I sat forward. "You've never said anything about this before."

"Remember that child shoplifting thing we had going in

the spring? The one during the teachers' strike? I'm still convinced he was a major player in that game."

For two months the mall had been overrun with kids, mostly kids from ten to thirteen years old. Mothers would send them over with a couple of dollars to get them out of the house for a few hours. What the mothers didn't realize was that, in addition to their couple of bucks, a lot of the kids came with a list of things to steal. Things that ranged from clothes to electronics to jewellery.

It was quite a professional setup—small scale but well organized. Most stores don't prosecute kids that young, and the entrepreneurs behind the scheme knew it. They even gave the kids a list of excuses to give their parents if the stuff was found in their room at home. The kids made pocket money, the middle man made a bit more and the final recipient got bargain prices.

"I just wasn't able to prove anything," Helen went on, "but I'm pretty certain he processed the stuff the kids were stealing. I mean, how many twelve and thirteen-year-olds do you usually see going in and out of a flower shop? We watched that store like hawks, but never saw them exchange anything except conversation, and not a lot of that.

"I've never said anything, because it's still an open investigation. The police are having problems, because the parents don't want to believe their children would do such a thing, and the kids sure aren't talking."

She put down her soup mug, stood up and rewrapped the bath towel she was wearing. Her thick black hair, still wet from the shower, made strange little patterns in the talcum powder on her shoulders. No recessive genes there.

"I guess whether Menard was involved or not is moot now, though, isn't it?" she continued. "And another thing, he was awfully tight with that guy who ran the liquor store. The one who was convicted last year of running the teen prostitution ring. They spent a lot of lunch hours together. Every time I spotted them with their heads together, I wondered what they were cooking up." Helen sighed. "Anyway, that's all beside the point now. The liquor store guy's in jail, and Menard's dead. I gave George my Security Log for the past year so he could go over it. Menard's mentioned in it quite a lot, and coincidentally, so is today's other victim, Jones, the one in hospital. In fact, I'm more concerned about the trouble that's going to come from him."

"Why?" I asked. "At least he's still breathing in and out."

"And that's about all he's doing. Just before we went into a mini-meeting in Graham's office, my precinct sources told me, off the record, that it might be best if he just slips away. He got shot in the back of the head and, apparently, the doctors aren't predicting much of a future for him if he does survive."

"Did you tell them that at the meeting?"

"Are you crazy?" she asked. "You know whose son he is, don't you?"

I looked at her. She nodded, and I knew.

"Oh, God. That Jones."

"That Jones," she agreed. "Stephen Jones Jr., whose father, Councillor Stephen Jones Sr., is the biggest thorn in the side of this shopping centre, what with his watchdog Citizens' Advisory Committee and his constant carping about inadequate security, inadequate lighting, ineffective management, etc., etc.

"Bob Graham was upset enough for one night and, who knows, medical miracles have happened before. No doubt his condition'll come out at the meeting tomorrow, but it won't be from my mouth.

"You know, of course," she took another sandwich, a sure sign she was upset, "my job's been on the line a number of times due to Jones. He's never got over the fact that I banned his son for three months last fall. Remember I caught the little shit hassling the models in the fashion show? His remarks when they were on the runway were bad enough," she said, "but fixing the tent so's he could watch them changing, specially after he'd just been warned, was too much."

I nodded, thinking back to all the times the Councillor's son had caused us grief, then squirmed his way out of it because of his father's position. One of Helen's staff had caught him cutting a slash in the curtains of the models' change tent during the fashion show, and that was the last straw for her. He was out, she'd said, and told Bob if he overruled her because of Jones Sr., she'd quit. The Councillor had lost that one.

"Mind you," Helen added, "the father thinks he's God's gift to women, so maybe the son comes by it naturally. God help any girl who gets caught up with him. In fact, I'm still convinced it was Junior who slashed my tires last month. Him or a couple of his buddies. Come to think of it, he's probably in the log book even more times than Menard."

Helen's tires get slashed about five times a year. It's part of her job agreement that the mall management replaces them. The vandalism is usually done by kids who get banned or thrown out for a variety of reasons. The mall owners' policy is that anyone caught in the mall while they're under a ban is charged with trespassing, and they're pretty strict about enforcing it. The offender ends up in court, where he or she has to explain to a judge why the ban shouldn't be permanent. Unfortunately for Helen, she's the one who represents the owners in court so, as far as the culprit's concerned, it's her fault they're in trouble.

"The Councillor's latest kick is contract security." Helen

did a wicked parody of Stephen Jones Sr.'s high-pitched nasal voice. "'My wife works at that new mall north of here and they've got contract security and they don't have the problems you people do.' The fact that they don't have any customers, either, doesn't seem to factor in. He's only gunning for me 'cause of his kid. You can bet he's going to have a field day with today's performance.

"Asshole." She hitched her towel a bit higher, "I still kick myself for not having his precious son formally charged with tire-slashing. I couldn't have proved it, but it might have cooled both of them down a bit."

She got up and began picking up our empty dishes. "Anyway, as you know, the cops finished up about six, six-thirty and other than George keeping a few people back for a second interview, most everybody cleared off home. I let my staff go half-an-hour or so later. No point in making any of them stay. The police left a team of people on watch overnight, inside the mall as well as out in the parking lot."

"What kept you so late, then?" I asked. "Making eyes at Anderson again, are we? I thought that was finished."

"Well, it was, but my mother always said you should never close a door you might want to go back through, and I'm going to need all the support I can get on this. If Jones Sr. gets his way, I'll be in deep shit for sure if these murders aren't solved and solved fast. I aim to use any sources I've got from my days at the cop shop, and old boyfriend or not, George is in charge of the case.

"Think about it, Jenny, if the shootings aren't cleaned up in record time, we'll be able to have a bowling tournament in the mall for the staff and the tenants, 'cause there sure won't be any customers getting in the way. Have you thought what next week's going to be like?"

I put away my knitting, took the bags off my knees and stood up. "I can see the headlines now," I said. "Something along the lines of 'Shop Till You're Dropped' maybe or 'Best Buys in Town—If You Live Long Enough?' Maybe I could run a special 'Dodge the Bullet and Win a Pizza' promotion. That would really have them lined up at the doors, don't you think?"

"God, that mouth of yours just keeps on going, doesn't it? That's not funny. Two people dead, one nearly, I've had a rotten day, I'm exhausted and you're trying for laughs?"

"It's just self-preservation." I put the corn back in the freezer. "That's all. Self-preservation. If I don't laugh, at least a little, I'll cry. My day's been rotten too, you know. I might not have had to deal with bodies and cops and coroners, but I lost Santa, and that's just as bad.

"What's more, who do you think the tenants are going to come after, starting Monday? And when you've answered that, who do you think Graham's going to throw to the press, starting tomorrow? And then, when you've answered that one, tell me who's going to have to come up with something to get the fucking customers back in the mall?"

"Suzy Q, that's who," she said, and we both burst out laughing. "Okay, that's it. If we're laughing at a double murder, it's time to hang it up. I'm for bed."

She put the dishes in the sink and, limping a bit, headed for the back staircase that went from the kitchen up to her bedroom.

"What's wrong with your feet?" I asked.

"Just my new shoes pinching a bit. Wouldn't you know I had to wear them today of all days?"

I stared at her. I was suddenly very cold.

"What's wrong, Jenny?" she knew immediately something had changed.

"Shoes. My God, Helen, shoes."

"What about shoes?"

"There was a man in my office this morning, Dick Simmons. He wanted his shoes fixed. He was furious at Gord in the shoe repair shop. Didn't like his repair job. What with Santa and the pumpkins and the shootings, I forgot all about it till now. The conversation got pretty ugly, and he made threats, Helen. He threatened to shut down the centre. 'Fix your whole fucking mall' I think was the way he put it."

"Do the police know about this?"

"No, I told you, I forgot till just this minute."

"Didn't they question you in the Food Court? I thought they talked to everybody. Surely you would have remembered it then?"

I shook my head. "I guess they missed me when I went upstairs to get my knitting. Anyway, that doesn't matter. I've remembered it now. I figured he was just blowing steam and would cool down over the weekend. He's going to bring the shoes back on Monday. At least, that's what I told him to do. I thought about him for a flash when I saw all the cops around the bodies, but it seemed so absurd, I guess I just forgot about it."

"It does seem a bit extreme for a customer complaint, but who knows? Anyway, it's not up to us to make that judgement." She picked up the phone. "We'll tell Anderson and let him deal with it. I doubt we'll get him tonight, though."

I hauled my hot water bottle out from under the sink and ran the tap. If ever there was a night I needed it to hug, this was it. Maybe I'd put on a flannelette nightie too, and maybe those nice, soft bedsocks I'd knitted last year. A girl needs all the help she can get when things are getting away from her.

"Well, I didn't think so." Helen hung up the receiver. "But I left a message for George telling him it was urgent he talk to you tomorrow before the meeting. That way he can get somebody on it first thing."

"Should I go to the station?"

"He'll be at the mall. From what I gathered earlier, he's going to give us an update on the situation as it sits now. At least he'll give us as much information as they're prepared to release. Probably won't amount to much more than we know already.

"Well, goodnight, Jenny. Make sure the fire's tamped down before you go to bed."

She headed for the stairs for the second time, then stopped and turned, a hand on the banister and one foot on the bottom step. "What do you mean you lost Santa?"

I looked at her for a minute then just closed my eyes. "Not now, Helen. I'll tell you tomorrow."

Four

I was kneeling by the kitchen door lacing up my sneakers when Helen came downstairs the next morning.

"It's only six-thirty, for Crissakes," she said. "Only people who can't sleep get up at six-thirty."

Helen, for all her insistence on being at the peak of fitness, can't get up in the morning without a minimum two whacks at the snooze-button and a lot of dreadful muttering while she staggers around looking for the bathroom. Last month, she'd woken up and found herself out on the balcony three times, so I brought home some huge foam core arrows left over from a promotion and laid them out leading from her bed to the shower. She wasn't amused and, though she denies it, I know it cost me a couple of her home-cooked meals.

"I slept," I said. "In fact, I slept like a baby, didn't toss once, didn't turn once. I feel great." I stood up and bounced around a little to prove it. "I tell you, Helen, you've got to get a hot water bottle. Does the trick every time."

"Why're your shoes on? It's hardly time to be leaving yet, or have I missed something here? And don't tell me George phoned already," she said. "I know from experience that he won't be up yet, unless he worked all night."

"No, I haven't heard anything. I just thought, seeing as I feel so feisty, that I'd start jogging with you today, and then we'll go on over to work and give George a hand solving these murders. I mean, how hard can it be? And you've been after me for a while to get exercising, so I figured this morning's the time."

"Well, you figured wrong, cowboy."

She went over to the coffee maker, plugged it in and started doing whatever it is you do with those things to make a pot of joy juice. Being a tea drinker myself, I've never even tried to figure out how it works. Even serving my guests instant coffee seems more civilized than trying to deal with something that spits and hisses.

She walked to the table, mug in hand, and dragged a chair over to prop up her feet. There was a band-aid on each heel.

"I'm not going jogging today. I'm too tired, my feet hurt and I'm too upset and, if that's not enough for you, I just don't feel like it. So put that in your smike and pope it, I mean your poke and smipe it. Oh, shit, you know what I mean."

She drained her mug and got up to pour a refill.

"Besides, you just can't rush out and jog three miles, Jenny. These things have to be worked up to. First, you do warm-ups, and I don't mean with a hot water bottle. Then you walk a bit, you jog a bit and then you walk a bit more. Then you have a cooling down period. It's not a case of simply charging out the door and up the road, you know. There's an art to jogging, and I'm not in the mood to show you today, so just forget it."

"Okay," I said.

On a driving trip through Texas last year, I'd noticed the highway signs read "Don't Mess With Texas." Dealing with Helen in the morning is often like that, so I just picked up my knitting and went through to the front room to wait for George's phone call.

•

When the phone rang, it wasn't George but a desk sergeant telling me to meet Inspector Anderson at eight o'clock at the west entrance of the shopping center.

I got there a few minutes before the appointed time and drove around the parking lot to scope it out. There were a couple of police cars at the main entrances, and I saw two media vans, but not much else was going on. It just looked like a typical Sunday morning, mostly quiet and deserted, since the shopping center doesn't open before noon on Sundays.

I guess the police had stopped any sightseers from nosing around, but the word was sure to have spread by now. They'd be here in droves later. Somebody else's trouble always acts like a giant magnet, and it was a sure bet that lots of people who turned up today would be the same ones that couldn't wait to leave yesterday. Whether they'd get inside or not was another story.

I found George talking to a couple of his men just outside the doors at the west side of the parking lot. He beckoned me over and introduced the men as Detectives Hobart and Bartolo.

They were both about my height, five-foot-eight give or take, and just about as skinny, although I sensed a wiry, controlled strength in both of them. Dressed in matching navy blue blazers and grey slacks, they each had dark, curly hair styled in what could only be a regulation cut, and they both wore black, solid-looking shoes polished to the nth. Pete and Repeat, I thought. They were so alike, there was no way it was accidental. I was tempted to take them home and stand them on the mantle.

I swallowed hard. "Pleased to meet you, Detectives," I said. "I'm Jenny Turnbull, Promotion Director for Rosewood. I take it you're working on our shooting?"

One of them said "Ma'am", and the other one touched his head in a kind of salute.

They both had better-than-average good looks, but the more I looked at them, the more I felt a menace in their similarity, as if they were saying "if one of us doesn't get you, the other one will."

"Well, Jenny," said George. "What's this about? I got a message that you have urgent information about what happened here yesterday?"

"Well, I don't know if it's directly related to the shooting. Probably not, but here it is." I launched into the story about my meeting with Dick Simmons to the three of them. When I got to the bit about his promise to "fix the whole fucking mall", three pairs of eyebrows went up, and Pete and Repeat looked at each other.

Halfway through my recital, George shoved his hands in his pockets, and by the time I finished, the skin on his normally handsome face had tightened, and his mouth was a thin slash.

"His address?" His voice was terse and came through his teeth.

"I don't know," I said. "I didn't ask. I just told him to come back on Monday."

"You suggesting we wait till Monday to speak to this man, Miss Turnbull?"

Uh-oh, he's getting formal, he must be really angry, I thought. Play it straight here, Jenny.

"Of course not, Inspector," I looked up at him, way up. "I'm simply telling you I didn't ask for his address, but it's probably on his repair ticket. Gord Jenkins'll have that. I brought the tenant emergency list with me." His hand appeared and darted out, grabbing the list. "Gord's home phone number's on it."

George shoved the paper at Hobart hyphen Bartolo and jerked his head towards a car sitting at the curb.

"Get Jenkins and then get Simmons. I'll be in a meeting for one hour. Have them waiting when I get out."

He turned and walked off without so much as a glance or a word in my direction. Determined not to walk behind him, I got back in my car and circled the lot a few times before parking and going upstairs. I'd seen George in a snit before. It wasn't pleasant, and even though I was willing to concede it might be somewhat justified this time, I didn't want to be in his line of sight before he'd had time to get over it.

•

The management offices boast a large conference room off the main suite with seating capacity for sixteen around a solid teak table. The far wall, facing the door, is corkboard, and an architect's floor plan of the Food Court was pinned to it.

Someone had been in and set out filled water jugs, glasses, paper and pencils. Two coffee pots were full and sitting on warming rings on a credenza off to one side, with three plates of donuts beside them.

Bob Graham, Keith Armstrong and Anderson were already in the room, standing talking at the far end of the table. Helen came in just after I sat down. Her uniform, grey slacks, navy blazer and snow white shirtblouse looked particularly crisp this morning. She walked over without a glance at George and sat in the chair next to mine, handing me a brown paper lunch bag.

"Here's a couple of blueberry muffins. I made them just after you left."

"Thanks, Pocahontas," I said. And we were back on track.

"Who else is coming?" she asked.

"I'm not sure," I said. "I thought it was just the four of us and George, and we're all here, so I've no idea what the holdup is."

"How did your appointment go? What did he think about your shoe man—what's his name again?"

"Simmons. Dick Simmons. Let's just say I'm not your Inspector's favourite person at the moment." I told her what had happened outside and about Pete and Repeat being dispatched like a couple of hound dogs, which I guess, in a way, they were. "It really was stupid of me not to have remembered it sooner though, I'll give him that."

"Don't worry too much about it, Jenny. I know Hobart and Bartolo, and they're quite a team. If there's anything strange about Dick Simmons, they'll know it three seconds after they find him."

"Trust me, Helen, there's plenty strange, but who knows whether it's got anything to do with the shootings."

I looked up in surprise as the door swung wider, and in walked Michael Leung with Jim Evans, manager of Hart's Department Store, and Steve Walker from Williamson's, our other department store. As major players in Rosewood City Centre, Graham must have felt they should be privy to the update meeting. I just hoped he wouldn't let them sit in on the strategy decisions we had to make after George finished, or we'd be there all day.

Leung owned and operated a small imported giftwares store on the lower level and, as president of our Merchants Association, he rightly felt he had a duty to uphold the interests of the small independent retailers whose operating procedures didn't always agree with those of the large chains and department stores.

There's a standing resentment in the shopping center

industry about the weight a large, national tenant can bring to bear on the mall management, yet those same small retailers only lease space because the mall has the large retailers in it. They want to be in with the big guns, because they know the big guns bring in the customers. It's a kind of "damned if you do, damned if you don't" thing, when you're one of the little guys.

Bob Graham turned around and asked everybody to sit down. As usual, he was dressed in a three-piece suit and immaculately ironed white shirt. The rest of us tend to slack off a bit on a weekend if we're at work, but not Bob. He always looks like a page from some up-to-the-minute fashion mag. In his early fifties, Bob keeps his silver-streaked hair beautifully cut and styled, his nails manicured and always wears quiet but tasteful accessories. I call him 4M—Mr. Model Mall Manager—but never in his hearing.

But he's not a bad guy, and most of the time, he's a decent boss, as long as you remember the credo, "Get the Rent", which also translates as "Maximize the Mall." He figures even the floor space I use for promotions should be making money, and every now and then he calls a staff meeting to see if there's a way the Merchants' Association budget can be charged for it. It'll happen one day. It's only a matter of time.

Bob centred a notepad and pencil in front of him and cleared his throat.

"I've invited Mr. Leung, Mr. Evans and Mr. Walker to join us for the first part of this morning's meeting."

I breathed a silent prayer of thanks. So far, so good.

"In Mr. Leung's capacity as president of our M.A., he'll be a big help to us in communicating with the other tenants, and Jim and Steve, as the two largest employers in Rosewood City Center will, I'm sure, be able to help us maintain as normal an operating policy as possible during the next few days."

Dream on, I thought, looking at Leung, whose face had tightened at Bob's use of first names for the other two.

"And now I'll turn the meeting over to Duty Inspector George Anderson. Inspector Anderson is in charge of the official investigation into yesterday's unfortunate occurrence."

"Good term for it," Helen leaned over and whispered to me. "Two and a half murders, and he calls it an 'unfortunate occurrence'."

Bob looked our way. "Did you have something to say, Ms. Lemieux, before Inspector Anderson begins? Something we should all hear?"

"No, sir," she said. "Please go ahead."

"Thank you," he said. "Inspector Anderson?"

George elected to stand and drew himself up to his full six foot four. He cut an impressive figure. Handsome, with blonde curly hair, dark brown eyes and a body you just wanted to stroke, I could see why Helen had been taken with him in the first place. His looks were enough to attract any woman, and I think that had turned out to be the problem. On a social level, George was quite charming and enjoyed the attention that invariably came his way. I guess he enjoyed it a bit too much to suit Helen, who's the one-at-a-time type.

After living with him for just over a year, she'd called me one day and simply said, "I have to come and stay with you." I said okay, and that was that. Plain and simple. I hadn't asked the questions, and she hadn't volunteered the answers.

Because my job is a high-profile one in our community, I get invited to a lot of different functions, so I run into George quite often, and Helen stills sees a fair bit of him because of her numerous court appearances. From what I've seen recently, they appear quite relaxed and friendly with each other, so things must have progressed, but he always seems uncomfortable with me. I'm sure he believes I know all the intimate details of their relationship, and I can't think of a reason to tell him otherwise. It gives me an edge, and I like to have an edge.

George walked over to the wall, where the site plan of the Food Court was pinned up, and positioned himself in front of it. He looked for a minute at some papers he was holding, then put them down on the table.

"Good morning," he said. "As Bob has told you, I'm the Duty Inspector in charge of the investigation into yesterday's shooting. As such, I'm here to give you a short update on what we've been able to determine took place yesterday and give you such details as we feel won't compromise our investigation. I won't speculate, and I won't answer any questions."

This was going to be short all right. I opened my lunch bag and took out a muffin. 4M glared at me.

George put a finger on the Paul's Pizza location on the site plan. "At 11.33 a.m. on Saturday, October 31, my department responded to a 911 call from Helen Lemieux, your Security Chief. She reported that three people had been shot while sharing a table in the Food Court area of the mall, and she requested emergency response and assistance.

"Due to Ms. Lemieux's police background, she knew the importance of securing the area, and using her own staff, immediately blocked off the area in front of the particular food outlet, Paul's Pizza, where the shooting occurred. Thanks to her quick action, the crime scene was preserved as well as could be expected, considering it's a public area."

Helen scribbled on a piece of paper and slid it to me. *That won't hurt any when Jones comes calling.*

I hear you, I wrote back.

George went on.

"The Coroner pronounced two people dead at the scene, and the third victim, critically wounded, was rushed to hospital under police escort. His condition this morning remains critical. The deceased are Cathy Haggerty, co-owner of Haggerty's Wools, and Gerry Menard, manager of Sweethearts' Florists."

He glanced at the papers in his hand. "The wounded man is twenty-three year-old Stephen Jones Jr., the son of Councillor Stephen Jones who, from what I've been told by Mr. Graham here, is well known to all of you."

I gave a quick glance around the room. All eyes were on George, but it seemed that was all he had to say about Jones.

"We know the gun used was a .22 calibre target revolver—a highly accurate weapon with rapid fire and fast recovery. As yet, it has not been located. We know the shots were fired from a recessed door adjacent to the pizza place and, after questioning over a hundred and fifty potential witnesses who were eating lunch in the area, we know that nobody saw a thing.

"The door in question closes off a hallway that runs at the back of that side of the Food Court, and the closest thing we have to a statement is that one diner thinks she saw a hook pull it closed from the hallway side."

"A hook?" asked Jim Evans.

To his credit, he sounded quite normal. I, on the other hand, couldn't swallow my bite of muffin.

"Yes, sir," said George, "a hook."

"A metal hook?" Evans again.

"Yes, sir, a metal hook. Quite probably part of a Halloween costume. Possibly a pirate."

"Worn by our killer?" asked Bob.

"We don't know that, but we do know a large number of adults were in costume yesterday as well as the kids. In the space of three hours, for instance, during the interviews, my men questioned twenty-nine gorillas, fourteen aliens..." he looked back down at his notes "...four belly dancers, half-a-dozen bananas, two Jolly Green Giants, three Marilyn Monroes and one toffee apple. They also spoke to Elvis Presley, fifteen times."

He turned his back and coughed a couple of times into his hand.

Only in the shopping center business, I thought. Where else could you find eight adults sitting around a table having a serious discussion about murder in terms of aliens, Elvis and a toffee apple? Maybe a television talk show?

"The only other thing I have to add," George said, "is that due to certain factors which I won't go into, we're pretty certain this was not a random shooting."

He put down the pointer and walked over to stand behind his chair. "Mr. Graham has stressed the enormity of the impact these killings will have on your operation, particularly with your Christmas season only a couple of weeks away. I'm telling you this today in the hope that the impact may be lessened somewhat if your merchants and the general public understand we have no reason to believe a killer is stalking the customers in Rosewood City Center.

"That information was not given to the press yesterday, of course, since what we know now only came to light late last night. There's another press conference scheduled for later this evening, and they'll be informed then. They will, naturally, only be given the same statement I just gave you and, although I can't order you not to talk to them, I strongly suggest when you're approached that you refer them to me in all matters regarding the incident."

At the last part, he looked directly at me. So did Helen,

Bob and Keith. The four of them knew I'd been seeing quite a bit of Jim Masters lately, and while Helen thought it was an okay thing, it grated on Bob and Keith.

Jim was the publisher of our local paper, and Bob felt our relationship was somehow a conflict of interest, something to do with Rosewood being the paper's biggest advertiser and me being the one who allocated the advertising budget. From thinly veiled remarks Keith dropped every so often, 4M had obviously enlisted his support.

I found it insulting, but this wasn't the time to get into it, so I just smiled at the room in general and took another muffin.

•

"That's a bit of good news anyway," Helen said.

We were in the washroom down the hall from the boardroom. Anderson and the three retailers had left, Bob and Keith were doing their morning once-around of the centre, then the four of us were to meet in Bob's office afterwards. Before the day started pecking, we had to come up with a game-plan on how to handle the tenants, the press and, most importantly, Stephen Jones. He could do us the most damage right now. Mall developers detest any kind of bad publicity, especially when they own other undeveloped land in the municipality— land that needs council approvals on every aspect of any proposed use. Our Head Office was no different in that the company held a number of large tracts slated for future construction. They'd be on Bob's case daily over this business.

"You mean the bit about it not being a random shooting?"

I pulled a comb through my hair, trying to get it to flatten down a bit, a hopeless job. No wonder it's on my list of things to hate. It frizzes up when a damp cloud goes by, and no matter how I have it styled, it's got a mind of its own. Most of the time, I just keep it cropped short, but I hadn't had time for a cut lately.

"Yeah," said Helen. "I wonder how they arrived at that so fast?"

"I don't know, but I did have a thought when Bob was glaring at me in there. We should see if Menard or Haggerty were behind on their rent. Bob would kill for that, y'know. Maybe he's our shooter."

She hit the button on the wall dryer, looked at me and said "Hook."

I gave up on the hair and stuck the comb in my pocket. "Yeah, you're right. Our impeccable boss wouldn't be caught dead as Long John Silver, would he?"

"Not in a million. Anyway, let's get to this meeting and see what's what."

Five

Bob closed the side door to his office and settled himself behind the desk. Like the rest of him, everything was lined up and matching. My office drives him crazy.

"Jenny," he's fond of saying, "a cluttered desk is the sign of a cluttered mind."

So what's an empty desk the sign of?

Keith came in through the door leading from the reception area carrying a coffee mug and stood against the far wall beside the escape hatch. The office wall facing Bob's desk has a row of curtained windows and a solid metal door that leads to the outer hall. He can see out, but people coming along the hall can't see in, so if he spots somebody he doesn't want to deal with, he simply scoots out the fire door. It's hard on Shirley, because she never knows whether he's there or not. She keeps trying to get him to give a couple of knocks on the wall if he's bolting, but he never remembers.

"Before we start plotting a strategy," said Bob, "I want to review and recap this morning's meeting."

Bob loves to "recap" everything. It must work for him, since he never forgets anything. Of course, the fact that he writes absolutely everything down doesn't hurt either. After a conversation with him, you can expect a memo within half-an-hour, outlining, in detail, what you had talked about. Today's was sure to be a three-pager, but that was okay. The habit keeps Shirley busy and saves the rest of us taking notes.

"Michael Leung will talk to the rest of the Board of Directors and give them the information we got today—the main part, of course, being that the police believe the shooting wasn't random. He'll ask those seven to each take a group of merchants and pass it along to them. Hopefully that will cover most of the tenants.

"Walker and Evans promised a staff meeting tomorrow morning with their department heads who, in turn, can talk to the employees, and that'll cover the majors. I'll call the chain store head offices and deal with them.

"Jenny, you handle the press—the two of us'll talk about that later—and you'll also, of course, talk to the merchants. We can't leave all of that to Leung. Keith'll help you there. Helen, see that your department liaises with the police and gives them every cooperation. The four of us should try to meet every morning till this is over.

"Remember, no matter who you're talking to, I want all of you to stress the 'not random' bit, though God knows, if it wasn't random, what was it?"

"Targeted." Helen looked over at me.

"Why? And which one?" Keith, whose personality and mannerisms lean to the practical, wasn't much of a talker. When he does speak, though, it's usually to the point.

I once heard him being reamed by a guy complaining about his car being towed from our parking lot. Keith pointed out that it'd been parked in the fire lane, but the man demanded that the mall pay the forty-five dollar fee to get his car back.

"No," said Keith, walking away. "Next time, though, phone ahead and we'll open the doors so you can drive right in and shop from your car."

Now he looked at me, too, I guess, because Helen was still looking at me, so I launched into the story of Dick Simmons, his shoes and his threats.

When I was about halfway through, Bob put up a hand. "Anderson told me about that, Jenny, but though he doesn't discount it yet, he seems to think it's a bit much for a dissatisfied customer, and I tend to agree with him. Let's wait to see what happens after the police speak to him. Mind you, I'd love it if he is the killer. It would sure—"

He was cut off mid-sentence by a thump that rattled the windows behind Helen's head. She jumped up and swung around. "Jesus, what the hell was that?"

Keith and I got to the door just as it burst open. Keith's forward motion took him full smack into the edge of it and his coffee mug flew up and back, splashing both of us with his drink.

Councillor Jones' large body followed the swing of the door and passed us in what would be known in rhino language as a charge. As he went by, I caught a quick glance of a badly rumpled suit, twisted tie and open shirt collar.

"Where's Graham?"

He kept moving, and it was obvious he didn't really want an answer, which was just as well. Keith and I were too busy holding our clothes away from our skin and trying to shake them out.

"You all right, Jenny?"

"I'm okay, but thank God it wasn't any hotter." I looked in dismay at my cream-coloured silk shirt. Scratch that one, I thought. "Keith, this looks like trouble. You follow him in while I get some towels."

"Call Security while you're at it." He started into the office. "Have a couple of the guys come up and sit in your office."

I took off down the hall and into the kitchen, grabbed a tea towel and mopped my shirt as best I could, then called Peter and told him what was happening. "Just have them hang out in my office for a while, Peter, in case things turn nasty."

Clutching a clean towel for Keith, I hurried back to Bob's office, not wanting to miss any more of the action than I already had. Near the door, I heard the Councillor shouting. "You're all responsible for my son's shooting, all of you. And especially her, with that Mickey Mouse security bunch."

Through the open door, I saw him point at Helen. When I walked in, he turned from his stand in front of Bob's desk and gestured towards me, his other hand flailing out. "And here's another one," he said.

I opened my mouth to ask "another one what?", but Bob gave a quick shake of his head, so I just shut it again.

Jones swung round to face Keith. They each did a little shuffle step to the right, circling like a couple of Rottweilers. Then his attention turned back to Bob, who was the only one seated. Helen stood over by the windows behind her chair, and Keith stood between her and Jones. Coffee dripped from his jacket onto the toes of his shoes. I walked over, handed him the towel and sat in the chair by the door where I'd been earlier.

The tirade continued, raw anger filling the room. "Call yourself management? Call yourself fuckin' management? What a joke that is. Just look at you! Four idiots who couldn't manage their way out of a paper bag. Well, it's not good enough for me. I'm telling you, Graham, something had better be done about this, and done now, or else."

He brought a fist down on Bob's desk, his face tight with emotion. His cheek muscles spasmed, and the veins in his neck were stretched to an impossible size, standing out like twists of knotted wire.

"The doctors say my only son might die today. My wife's

in shock, admitted to hospital last night under sedation, and I've just spent eighteen hours going from one bedside to the other."

His voice broke on the last few words, and he started raking through his pockets with angry jerks of his hands. The rest of us were rooted to our spots, and for a few seconds, the only sound was a sort of desperate rasping as Jones sucked in great gulps of air.

Bob stood up, took the white handkerchief from his breast pocket, walked around the desk and handed it to the distraught man.

"Please sit down, Stephen." He spoke quietly, one hand on the man's shoulder, the other gesturing to the small couch to the right of his desk.

Jones collapsed in a heap on the cushions and, without any more fuss, quite simply came apart. Elbows on his knees, he clutched his head in both hands and sobbed.

Keith disappeared from the office for a few minutes and returned with a glass of water, handing it to Jones. Helen and I looked at each other, at the walls, at Bob. Keith examined the furniture. I checked my shirt for stains. Helen lifted the curtains and looked through the glass, and Bob sat behind his desk, quietly straightening the pencils.

After a few minutes, the Councillor wiped his face and looked up. "I don't want my boy to die. I don't want my wife to suffer. I don't want to hurt like this. I just want to go back to yesterday morning. Everything was fine yesterday morning." His voice broke and the tears started again. "I want to hit somebody."

Bob got up and pointed from us to the door. Helen, Keith and I moved through it in unison.

"Take a few minutes alone, Stephen. I'll be back shortly."

Without a word, the four of us went down the hall to Keith's office. Nobody sat down. We all just kind of shuffled around and looked at the floor in sort of an embarrassed silence. Eventually Bob spoke.

"Okay," he said. "That's it for now. I'll see to Councillor Jones. I want to spend some time with him, anyway. Keith, you take over for me. We've still got a building to run, and Jenny, give me a couple of hours and meet me back here. We'll plan how best to handle the press. Simply referring them to Anderson won't work. We're going to have to talk to them."

He went to the door. "I also wanted to talk to you about the Thursday board meeting, Jenny, but I guess that's going to have to wait until tomorrow. I don't want to rush it. Christmas is too important."

•

In the hall, Helen and I let out the breath we didn't know we'd been holding.

"God," she said.

"Exactly," I answered.

She turned left towards the Security Offices. "See you at home later, Jenny."

"We'll see," I said. "I'm meeting Jim at his place. It's his turn to make dinner, so I'm really looking forward to it. But I'll catch up with you eventually."

"D'you think that's wise?" She stopped and came back. "Given the circumstances?"

"What circumstances?" I raised my eyebrows.

"Jenny, don't be cute. You know exactly what I mean. The shootings, the press, the police. Our boss, your position."

I held up a hand and counted off my fingers. "One, I can't

undo the shooting. Two, the press, as always, will do what the press is gonna do and three, I don't think the police are interested in my dinner date."

It was a date I wasn't that keen on keeping, but I wasn't about to admit that my interest in Jim was flagging slightly. He was a nice guy, and I'd enjoyed going out with him over the last while, but he took himself a tad too seriously for me.

"As for Bob Graham, my position is what it's always been. I'm for the separation of Church and State, and my job shouldn't depend on whom I do or don't socialize with. Besides, if you cut through all the altruistic bullshit, he's just twisted off 'cause I don't discuss the details of my relationships. It's got nothing to do with any "conflict of interest"; he's just plain nosy. And what's more, he's got Keith doing it, too. Every chance they get, they're quizzing me about who I'm seeing and how it's going. Doesn't matter that it's Jim right now; it was the same last year with Tom. It's a dick thing. Men are worse than women when it comes to wanting dirt, and it's making those two crazy because I'm not dishing any out."

I stopped for a breath, walked over and patted the shoulders of her blazer. "Sorry, matey, but you did ask."

"Well, it's your call," she said. "I'll see you when I see you."

She walked off up the hall, and I went the other way into the mall to find the kids and get the Halloween cleanup started.

We finished up in about an hour, and after the boys had gone, I went for double or nothing and left for home. I had no intention of discussing Jim with my boss that afternoon and had already decided to lie to him about Santa, so it made sense to just vacate the premises, as we say in this business.

I stopped by the Information Booth and told Mary, if she saw Bob, to say that "Jenny has left the building."

"Where shall I tell him you are?" she asked.

"Just tell him something came up, Mary, and I'll see him in the morning."

That should put his knickers in a knot, I thought. Even things out for glaring at me in the meeting.

I got out my car keys and headed out to the employee parking area through the service door at the south end of the Food Court. There were four police officers over by the Pizza outlet but, other than that, the place looked pretty normal. There weren't many customers, but then Sundays were never that crowded anyway. At least there weren't any dead bodies lying about either, so that was a plus.

The Chevy sat gleaming in bright sunlight. The weather always gives me a little jolt when I leave the mall. Working in an enclosed mall with no windows does that to you, makes you forget things like cold and hot, wet and dry. Inside is what our technical people refer to as a climate-controlled environment. Sometimes on the phone, a caller starts the conversation with "what d'ya think of this rain or snow or heat?", and you get the same little jolt because you're not aware of any rain or snow or heat.

Unlocking the car door, I climbed in and patted the dash. "Let's go home."

Six

I climbed the three flights of iron steps up to Jim's door thinking, not for the first time, that they'd really be a kick to negotiate in the winter. Oh, well, time enough to worry about that when the snow started to fly. Maybe there was some way of reaching his loft from inside the building which, in addition to Jim's living quarters, housed *The Weekly Times* newspaper operation.

Like most good newspaper people, Jim was joined at the hip to his job, so when the newspaper moved lock, stock and barrel to its current home—a former carpet factory—he had convinced the powers-that-be to let him take over the old third floor offices at the back, which were now converted into a chi-chi designer loft.

Benjamin Masters, Jim's grandfather, had started the paper some forty years ago as a small weekly tabloid. Over time, as the community grew, so did the paper, and though it still only published on Thursdays, it was now part of a chain of weeklies, was printed in full broadsheet format and serviced a cosmopolitan population of close to half a million. Somehow though, in spite of the enormous changes, *The Times* had maintained its image of a local community bulletin whose main responsibility was to report on happenings directly affecting the citizens it served. At least our shootings had happened on a Saturday, so the Rosewood story would be nearly a week old before it hit print. Hopefully that would dull the impact down a bit.

With the exception of three years at journalism school, Jim had worked at the paper all his life. Even during those years, he'd spent summers in the pressroom, all-nighters in the circulation department on Wednesdays and hung around the composing room on weekends watching the layout people work their cut and paste magic on the ad layouts. And now he was publisher. At forty-four years old, it was apparently some kind of record, and from what I'd heard around town, well-deserved.

Three years ago it had became obvious that the paper had outgrown its original space next to the old City Hall, and the operation was moved to the current building, with enough square feet on the ground floor to accommodate the administration offices as well as the editorial and advertising departments. There was even a separate section at the back, complete with loading docks, for the circulation crews.

I rang the bell and thought back to the first time I'd met Jim.

It wasn't the best start to a relationship, because I'd literally held all the cards but, over time, he'd learned to laugh about it. At least, I think he had. Jim's not given to laughing a lot, more's the pity.

When I'd first joined Rosewood Centre, Barb Donaldson, the advertising rep from the paper who handled the shopping centre account, had called to introduce herself and make arrangements to give me the grand tour of their facilities. In one phone call, lasting about four minutes, she managed to give me her name, marital status (single) and appearance (thin, blonde and sexy), her position at the paper, plus the fact that they appreciated our business and, as a commissioned salesperson, time was money, but she'd be only too happy to show me around. "Would tomorrow morning do?" She was getting her hair done in the afternoon.

Not wanting to burst her bubble by telling her I'd come up through the ranks of newspaper advertising, I'd duly met her the next morning and been given a whirlwind looksee at all the bells and whistles that were going to make our ads the absolute best in the country, which was a stupid thing to say because all our print advertising is prepared by a top-notch agency, and all Ms. Donaldson did was hand them to the composing room people to hot-wax onto a page flat. The tour ended in the cafeteria with my tour guide still talking non-stop and me feeling like the cereal which claims to have been shot from cannons.

She dropped some coins in a pop machine and got us each a soft drink. We took a table near a group who were playing the noisiest but fastest games of euchre I've ever witnessed. Cards were flying so fast the markings were just coloured blurs.

"How can they do that and still keep track?" I asked. "Look at them go."

"When you've only got fifteen minutes by the clock for your break time, and when you've got a Doberman for a press room foreman, you learn to be pretty fast. It's all part of the new world order." She took a pack of cigarettes from her pocket and held it out to me. We lit up, and she took a glass ashtray out of her purse, plonking it down on the table.

"What do you mean?"

"Well, we're not only in a new home now, but we've been computerized, digitized and…" she snorted "…sanitized, homogenized and, come to that, we're probably even pasteurized."

I raised my eyebrows.

"They spent so much money outfitting the building and laying in all the computer electronics and fancy furniture you can lay tongue to, we were all ordered to clean up our act.

Actually, it was more the editorial and composing room that was told to shape up."

She pointed at the ashtray and tucked a loose strand of hair behind her ear. "That should tell you something." Another snort. "As if having no ashtrays around would stop the smoking. Outright banning'll be next. You can forget any stereotypes you had of the hard-bitten newshound hunched over an old Underwood, cigarette ash dangling over the chest of his cardigan and shirt sleeves rolled up as he's madly ripping sheets of paper out the roller and throwing them over his shoulder while he's searching for just the right words. In today's world, there is no Underwood, there's a state-of-the-art computer over which you can't smoke in case the ash drops and screws up the keyboard. You can still wear the cardigan 'cause the building's so big it's always next to freezing, and you can even roll up your shirt sleeves, but there's no paper to rip out and even if there was, you're not allowed to throw it on the floor." A sigh this time. "Sometimes I wish I were a Promotion Director."

She stubbed out her cigarette and lit another one without missing a beat in her spiel.

"Got to get these smokes in before I introduce you to our publisher, Jim Masters, a.k.a. 'he who walks on water'." She glanced at her watch, put the ashtray and its contents back in her purse and dropped the newly-lit cigarette in her pop can. "And that's in about three minutes. Follow me." She stood up and was off down the hall, not bothering to turn around to see if I was behind her.

If Ms. Donaldson had given me any option, I might have chosen to go with her, but I've never taken kindly to being ordered about and besides, I was really put off by her diatribe, especially as we'd just met. The possibility of a working relationship with this gal was beginning to look a bit rocky. I have great respect for an assertive personality, but abrasive people just piss me right off, and I knew with certainty my mother wouldn't have liked her either. "A chippy", she'd have called her.

Thinking it was high time the said Ms. Donaldson was reminded of exactly who was on first, I picked up my drink and walked over to the euchre table where a new group had just sat down.

"Can anybody play?"

"And just who might you be?"

"I'm Jenny, and I'm just waiting for somebody."

"Well then, Miss Jenny, pull up a chair and let's deal these suckers."

When Mr. Masters eventually appeared in the cafeteria, as I knew he would, I'd smiled and waved to show who I was and where I was.

"Have a game, boss?" my new buddy Larry called out.

Jim walked to the table, sat down and dealt the next round. There was no sign of Ms. Donaldson.

•

The door to the loft swung inwards, and Jim stood framed in the opening. He made a wide, sweeping gesture and bowed deeply from the waist—a neat trick considering he held the doorknob in one hand, a glass of white wine in the other and a rose firmly clamped between his teeth. A burgundy apron swung forward as he bowed.

Norma Jean, his attack cat, was perched behind him on the newel post. I can't figure why some people say cats never meet your eye. This one always looked directly into mine, and the message was always the same: "Hands off—he's mine!"

"Good timing." Jim handed me the wine and the rose. "Dinner's almost ready. Come sit in the kitchen while I finish."

I silently conveyed my usual regards to the cat and dumped my jacket, purse and car keys on the hall chair.

Jim was dressed as usual in a designer shirt and custom-tailored slacks. This pair was exactly the same brown as his Italian loafers, which were exactly the same brown as his hair. This was his idea of laid-back casual clothing. Although not particularly handsome in a classic way, his grooming took him beyond that.

When he straightened up, I noticed his apron said "I'm a Liver Lover".

"Is that Norma Jean's pinny?" I asked.

Jim stopped abruptly and turned around with a startled expression. "Pinny? What's a pinny?" He went back, plucked Norma Jean off her perch and ran his hands over her back and down her legs. "Where do you see it?"

"Jim, relax. There's nothing wrong with the cat. A pinny's an apron. That's all, an apron." I pointed at the words on his chest. "I just wondered if you were wearing Norma Jean's apron."

"Very funny," He put the cat back on the post, patted her calico coat and hurried towards the kitchen. "Meanwhile, my masterpiece is probably burning. I've got a real treat for you. One of my family's all-time favourite dishes."

I grinned at Norma Jean, gave her a wave of my rose and a wide berth as I followed Jim down the hall into the kitchen.

The powerful and unique odor of liver came at me the minute I entered the room and, in a nanosecond, I went back twenty-plus years to being a kid and coming home from school to that smell.

My mother cooked liver once a week on the premise that "it's good for you, it strengthens your blood", and when that obviously made no impression, she'd trot out her standby stab at emotional blackmail, the one about kids starving all over the world.

Once, on liver night, as we were gagging it down, my sister suggested, in all innocence, that Mom could wrap her share up and send it to them. The response to that was a sharp slap, and dinner the following night was tripe, boiled with milk and onions.

After that, my sister and I made a solemn pact that when we grew up, neither of us would ever, ever eat liver or tripe ever again. As we recited our vow, we added kidneys plus everything else we hated but were made to eat.

"Cross my heart and hope to die," we said at the end and spat on the ground three times.

Taking a large gulp of wine, I sat at Jim's dinette table, as far away from the stove as I could. Through the archway on the opposite wall, I could see the dining room table beautifully set with elegant china, sparkling glasses and a snow-white damask cloth. In the centre, highly polished silver candlesticks held two white tapers, and a second red rose had been laid on one of the plates.

My heart sank while my stomach heaved. This, I thought, is going to have to be handled with some delicacy.

"Voilà!" Jim lifted the lid off a large frying pan with a flourish, held it out and brought it towards me.

"I can't eat that." It came out as a harsh bark.

Jim stopped in mid-stride. "What did you say?"

I jumped up and backed against the wall. "I said I can't eat that." So much for delicacy, but my gorge was rising. "I hate it, and I made a pact, you see, so even if I didn't hate it, I couldn't eat it because I made a pact, and when a person makes a pact, a person has to keep it."

Even to me, it sounded stupid. But there you go.

"But what about all…?" He shook his head as if to clear it. "…it's my mother's special recipe."

I looked at him. "Perhaps Norma Jean?"

Jim turned very quietly and walked over to the kitchen counter. He held the pan up, flipped it over and emptied the whole thing into the sink. He tapped it gently but firmly on the bottom to get it all out, laid it very softly on the counter top and swung back around. "Perhaps not."

He walked to the front hall, picked up the cat and went upstairs. "Goodnight, Jenny."

I drove straight to Bonnie's Burgers.

"No thanks, Jolene." I glanced at the nametag pinned to her breast pocket, holding a spray of white, frothy hankie in place. "I don't need a menu. I'll have a double burger, large fries and a side of onion rings."

"Gravy?"

"Of course."

"Drink?"

"Large cola."

"What's on the burger?"

"Everything."

Not much of a talker, our Jolene, but that was okay. Her timing, though, was perfect. Just as I wiped up the last of the gravy with the last of the fries, she was back.

"Dessert?"

"What's good?"

"Apple pie."

"Okay."

"Ice cream with it?"

"Of course."

Jolene was right. The apple pie was good and was made

even better by the ice cream. By the time I'd finished eating, I was almost over Jim's dismissing me so rudely. Almost, but not quite. In my opinion, he'd totally overreacted. Surely the least he could have done was let me explain before I was bounced. Oh, well, his loss.

I contributed a healthy sum towards Jolene's retirement fund and practically skipped my way out of Bonnie's feeling like a new woman. It's great what a healthy dose of piping hot, lip-smacking grease does for my ego.

Not wanting to lose my born-again glow and not ready to go home just yet, I decided to drive over to the hospital and find out how the Jones family was faring. The scene in Bob's office that morning flashed back into my mind. Replaying the Councillor's deep concern for his wife and son, together with his obvious distress, made me wonder if Helen and I had been misreading him all this time. But then I went back a little further to all the problems he'd caused us in the mall over the years and decided we hadn't. He was a bad-tempered bully, and his son was a little shit, as Helen said, even if he was near death.

I did feel bad for Jones Sr. right now, though, and I'm sure Bob, Keith and Helen did, too. Maybe we could have a truce for the time being, which was probably what Bob was trying to arrange after we had left him alone with Jones, and it would likely further the cause if I visited his wife and son.

That's me, always thinking.

•

Our local hospital is a sort of mutant building. It started life as a squat, two-story red brick building, pretty utilitarian but adequate and even modern for the times. Over the years, as the town grew up, so did the hospital. Fundraisers were held, wings were added on all sides and then, as money came in, those wings grew wings. The original roof came off next, and two extra floors were put on the old part of the building. It looks like the work of some architect gone daft, and if you unknowingly enter at the opposite end to where you want to be, you may as well pack a lunch.

I parked the Chevy as far away from other cars as I could, hoofed my way across the parking lot, and went in the front door to the bank of reception desks, stopping first at the gift shop for a bunch of fresh flowers.

It took all of three minutes at the Patient Inquiry desk to find out how the younger Jones was doing. A woman with Hospital Auxiliary embroidered on her pale blue uniform tapped a few keys on her keyboard and gave me the scoop in a clipped, tight voice. According to her records, he was still in Intensive Care, his condition was still critical, he was still under round-the-clock police guard and no, I couldn't see him.

I stood my ground.

"Was there something else?"

"Yes, as a matter of fact," I said. "I would like the room number for a Mrs. Stephen Jones."

Her fingers flew back and forth, entering in the name. "Third floor, private room. You'll have to see the head nurse on that floor."

I got off the elevator just as Councillor Jones was walking away from the nurses' station, tie and suit jacket hanging from a hand. Bits of his hair stuck out in tufts where he'd pushed it back through his fingers, and from the look of him, he hadn't washed or shaved seriously for quite some time.

After a couple of indecisive steps back and forth, he said something over his shoulder to a nurse and headed in my direction, pulling up short when he saw me.

"Turnbull."

I nodded, although it hadn't been a question.

"What the hell are you doing here?"

From across the hall, he'd been the epitome of a distraught man, but standing in front of me, his body language and stance said otherwise.

"Well, Mr. Jones…" unlike Bob, I couldn't get my mouth around his first name, "…well, sir, I just wanted to pop in and see how your son and your wife were doing. I knew, of course, that I couldn't get in to see him, but I feel so badly for them, actually for all of you…and thought maybe a little visit with Mrs. Jones…" I held the flowers forward, "…you know, pay my respects…perhaps a distraction…?"

I left it dangling, not quite sure of what else to say.

He turned away and punched the elevator button a couple of times. "Forget it." He hit the buttons again. "She's in no shape to see anyone, and even if she was, for Christ's sake, what makes you think she'd want to see anybody from your mall? *Especially* from your mall?"

He shot me a look and pointed at the flowers. "What're you looking for, Turnbull? Absolution? You think playing nice-nice to my wife'll make her forget your mall almost killed our son? And might yet."

So much for the guy I'd felt so sorry for this morning.

He jumped when the elevator arrived with a ping, and the doors opened. We rode down together in absolute silence. He stared at the floor and I stared at him, hardly able to believe I'd just been bounced for the second time in as many hours. I left the flowers at the reception desk. He stalked off towards the Intensive Care Unit.

Outside, the skies were crystal clear, but the temperature had dropped considerably. Starting the car up, I gave a fleeting thought to paying a sympathy call on Cathy Haggerty's family but then realized it probably wasn't such a good idea. Tomorrow would be better, or maybe I would even wait until the funeral. Shirley would have the details about that in the morning.

After being so thoroughly trounced by both Jim and the Councillor, I could feel a filthy mood coming on. Heading for home seemed the best option. I'd light a fire, make a pot of strong tea, then just sit and knit. If Helen was home, maybe I'd try to convince her to burn some sweetgrass to help me regroup.

Since the house was empty when I got home, there was no one to bitch to about my disastrous evening with Jim and the Councillor. I lit a fire, put the kettle on and then found we'd run out of tea, added to which I couldn't knit any more on Helen's sweater without the new wool whose supplier was now in the morgue. None of this improved my mood one iota, but there's no point in sulking if nobody's around to appreciate it, so I just sucked it up and went to bed.

Seven

I got to work somewhere around seven on Monday morning. Swinging the Chevy off the exit ramp, I headed for my usual spot. The parking lot was pretty deserted. At that hour, all you see are a few cars belonging to either the early shift maintenance or security people. Like everyone else who worked at the mall, I was expected to park at the far end of the lot and leave the prime space for customers, standard procedure in our business. Other than a couple of coffee and donut shops, Rosewood doesn't officially open for business until ten, so our designated area is always quiet in the early hours.

Today was no different, except for the body of a man lying stretched out on the ground beside the curb.

I yanked the steering wheel hard left and slammed both feet on the brake pedal. The car swung around almost a hundred and eighty degrees, shuddered a couple of times and stopped no more than two or three feet from the prostrate figure.

"Not again!" I was yelling louder than the tires were screeching. "Jesus Christ, not again!"

I punched down the door locks and opened the window an inch or two. "Help! Somebody help!"

The corpse rolled onto its stomach and, backside in the air, got up on all fours. Pushing backwards with an obvious effort, he eventually got to a standing position, bent his knees and stuck a hand between his legs to tug at the crotch of his coveralls. The front and sleeves were streaked with yellow, and there was a large smear of the same colour on the ground where he'd been lying. I spotted another one beside a paintbrush about three feet away.

He lumbered forward a couple of steps, bent down and shoved his face up to the window. His cheeks were mottled with jagged patches of reddish purple, and a vein above his left eyebrow jumped to its own beat. He grabbed the top of the window with fingers that looked like a pound of pork sausages.

Scrambling over to the passenger side, I clawed on the floor for my tire iron. (I call it the Equalizer.) It lives under the front seat, poised for situations just like this. Not that I've ever had to use it, but you never know.

"Are you fuckin' nuts?" he screamed. "You almost fuckin' killed me!"

"You're alive!"

"No shit!"

"You're painting the curbs!"

"No shit!"

"You looked like a body. A real body."

He straightened up, went back a couple of steps and threw up his hands in a gesture of disbelief. I could see a Rosewood Centre patch stitched to the chest of his coveralls with the name "Tiny" embroidered underneath the logo.

Of course, I thought. What else?

Why do people give out these cutesy nicknames and, even more strange, why do the recipients seem to like them? This guy was as wide as he was long and must have weighed in around two-eighty, most of it in front. Tiny he wasn't. If that belly had been on a woman, she'd be at least three weeks overdue.

A red pickup truck came tearing around the corner and pulled up behind me. Ed Spratt, our maintenance super, jumped out and came to the Chevy window.

"What's happening here? I could hear you shouting all the way in the shed." He looked at the tire iron. "You all right, Jenny?"

I nodded and sat up, sliding my defense back under the seat.

He spun around to Tiny. "What's going on? What'd you do? Why's she got the Equalizer out?"

That took me by surprise. I was aware most of the staff knew about it, but not what I called it. Still shaken, I got out of the car on the opposite side from the two men and leaned on the hood.

Tiny thrust out his chin, hands on hips and feet splayed. "What did I do?" His voice went up the scale. "She almost fuckin' killed me, and you're asking what did I do?" He drew himself up from toes to scalp, all five foot three or four of him, loving it. "I'm lying here paintin' the curb like you told me to, and she comes harin' in off the ramp, slams on the brakes and starts screaming for help. So I get up to see what's wrong and next I know, she's threatening me with a tire iron and saying I looked like a body. Fine start to a new job this is."

Ed's mouth was a thin line, and he was looking pretty pale. That scared me more than Tiny's screaming had.

It's common knowledge around the centre that Ed has a dicky heart which needs to be fitted with a pacemaker. I'm not sure what the exact medical condition is, but the symptoms are frightening. Every once in a while, his face turns stark white, and for a long moment, he can't catch his breath.

We'd all feel better if he gave in to the surgery, but Ed's a stubborn old coot. Says if he's going to peg it, he might as well do it at work as anywhere else and besides, it had only happened twice this year, hadn't it?

I came around the grill fast, but Ed waved me off.

"I'm okay. Really." He turned to the somewhat subdued Tiny. "I'll explain later. For now, just gather up your stuff and forget about the painting until tomorrow. Cars'll be arriving soon. I'll meet you back in the yard in a minute, get you started on something else."

Tiny shrugged and starting gathering up his gear. He wasn't so scary now that he'd quietened down a bit. His skin was back to all one colour, and he was actually beginning to look like a semi-normal person. As he walked off, he turned and looked at me over his shoulder. "Nice car, though."

"No shit," I answered.

I watched for a minute as he made his way across the lot. There was something familiar about that figure, although I knew with certainty that I'd never met him before today. You wouldn't forget meeting Tiny in a hurry.

But there was something.

Ed waited while I parked the car, then we headed for the entrance doors while he gave me the skinny on his newest employee. The man had shown up last week, desperate for a job and willing to do anything.

"He's really quite a decent guy, Jenny. Lives at home and looks after a disabled father. Got laid off from his mechanic's job a coupla weeks ago, and they told him to come see me. They gave him a good reference, too, said he's dependable and a hard worker and they were sorry to let him go but, like a lot of places, they're feeling the pinch and had to tighten up."

"But he was lying full length on the ground, Ed. Full length. That's what got me. I thought he was another dead body for our collection."

"I figured that," he said quietly. "But think about it for a minute. You saw him. With that stomach, he's too fat to sit on the ground and paint at the same time. He can't lean forward when he's down that low, and he sure can't do it on his knees, and we don't have a dolly he can fit on.

"There's a coupla miles of curb in this parking lot, you know. I guess lying on his side and inching his way along is the only way he can handle it, and so long as it gets done, I don't care how."

He got out his keys, unlocked the doors and held one of them open.

"How come you're having the curbs done now, anyway?" I asked. "It's November already. I thought Spring was the time for outside work?"

"Well, you know the boss. Some of the tenants are complaining about common area charges again, and every time they get really antsy, he decides to tart up some small bit of the mall to justify the operating budget. Guess he figures the curbs'll do it this time, even though they're gonna be covered up with snow in another few weeks."

In the shopping centre business, costs for cleaning, maintenance and repairs to the "common area" are worked out on a dollar figure per square foot basis and charged to the tenants. The major stores have a cap on their costs, and that just adds another gripe to small merchants' lists, but that's life in our industry.

Ed walked with me to the foot of the middle escalator.

"Got time for a tea, Ed?"

"Sure."

He flipped up a little cover in the floor and keyed the escalator to start. The motor hummed quietly, and the rubber handrail nearest to us came around with a bunch of multi-coloured stickers on it. As they went past, I saw they all had smiling pumpkin faces above the name of one of the stores. Ed sighed and passed a hand over his hair.

"Here we go again. Are they ever gonna get the message not to give out these things, Jenny?" He leaned over and pushed the stop button. "Now I'll have to get someone to scrape them off, and you can bet if they're stuck on this escalator, they're on the other two. Probably all over the washroom walls as well. Last time, they were stuck to the toilet seats too, and that took two men a whole day to clean off."

He shrugged and pulled a walkie-talkie out of his back pocket. "No wonder they gripe about CAM costs. Serves them right, if you ask me."

He held the radio up to his mouth and pushed the side button. "Manny, send the new guy over to the middle escalators and tell him to bring a putty knife and a paint scraper." The radio crackled. "Yeah, the sticker brigade's been at it again. Give him a set of keys. In fact, you may as well give him a set for the washrooms while you're at it. I'll meet him here and get him started."

He turned the motor on again so I could make my way up to the office. So much for tea.

•

Keith and Bob were in the kitchen brewing coffee. They both looked slightly surprised to see me.

"Something wrong?" I plugged in the kettle, got out my Brown Betty teapot, rinsed it out under the hot water tap and laid a couple of tea bags on the tray beside it.

"It's just that Keith heard you telling Helen yesterday that you were seeing Jim last night, so we figured you might be a little late this morning." Bob said. He gave a little smirk in Keith's direction. "Did you have a nice night?"

"Wonderful, thank you." I smiled and got out my favourite china cup, sugar and milk, added the teapot and filled it from the kettle. "And now, if you'll excuse me…"

"Hold on a minute." Bob took his ever-present appointment book and pen from his inside jacket pocket. "We're having our mini-meeting about the shooting situation at 9:30, and then I have a meeting at Head Office. Should be back just after lunch."

He scribbled down a few notes. "Let's say you and I meet at two in my office re the whole Christmas thing, Jenny. I really want to get to that."

"Two o'clock sounds good."

Balancing the tray with one hand, I unlocked the door to my office and shoved it open. A dozen foam pumpkins smiled at me from a pyramid pile in the middle of the desk. A note, in Helen's handwriting, was propped up in front of one of them reading *Good morning. Guess you and the boys forgot this bunch.*

I loaded them into the shopping cart I keep in the corner for just this sort of thing, threw in some other thing-a-me-jigs and geegaws that I wouldn't need again this year and pushed the whole lot down the hall to my main storage room.

Figuring the next couple of hours would be relatively quiet, I caught up on some paperwork, decided arbitrarily not to have a fashion show next Spring and wrote *Panic re S.* on every line of my list of things to do for Tuesday. That still gave me two days before the Board meeting. Besides, if I could lie to Bob this afternoon—which I had every intention of doing—and he swallowed it, I could, with impunity, present the same lie to the Directors. I slid the list under the desk blotter and started to make up time sheets for my kids for their weekend work. Next came the cheques to go with them and a couple more to cover the DJ and the pumpkin farmer.

I shuddered when I wrote that one up, thinking of all his produce heaped in the garbage compactor. When the kids and I were chucking them in the bin yesterday, I had a fleeting thought that I could at least make a couple of pies or maybe give them to somebody, but then, who the hell would want them?

"Good morning, Jenny." Shirley stood in the doorway, coffee mug in hand. "Anything important you need me to do?"

"Hi, Shirl. Come on in and sit down for a minute." I shuffled through the papers I'd been working on and gave her most of them. "Could you see that these cheques, especially the ones for the boys, get co-signed by Leung today, and give them a phone call after school so they can pick them up? I've padded the hours a bit. They did such a good job, they deserve a little extra. The others can go in the mail."

I pointed to the rabbit suits on top of the filing cabinet. "The rental company'll pick those up this morning. I'll probably be in Bob's office, so just leave their invoice on my desk. And at some time today, would you find out what you can about the funeral arrangements for Cathy Haggerty and Gerry Menard? We have to make a showing."

Shirley, unflappable as usual, made a few notes on her steno pad and stood up. "I'll get to the cheques first thing, but the phone calls might have to wait and, if I were you, I'd be prepared for an onslaught today. Sales figures, remember? It's the first of the month."

"Oh, God," I said. "So it is. With all this other business, it went right out of my head."

All tenants are required to hand in their sales figures along with the rent cheque for the previous month, preferably on the first but certainly no later than the third day of the next month. The only exceptions are the majors, who don't report sales figures, and those stores whose cheques are paid through a head office, although even they have to hand in sales figures.

Shopping centre rent is calculated on a dollar figure per square foot which is determined at the time of the offer to lease. There's normally a base rent plus a percentage of sales in excess of an amount projected for the sales for that particular type of business. At the end of the year, the accounting people figure out if the tenant has paid too much or not enough, then the dollars are adjusted, and the store either gets a rebate or is billed accordingly. In the meantime, the owner/developer gets the use of the money over the spread of the year.

"Don't bother about my copies of the sales figures this month, Shirley. I'm sure Halloween made a difference to them all right, but not one I'll want to crow about."

As Promotion Director, I don't get involved in rent collecting, but I do get a copy of the sales figures so I can compare them to the same month from last year. If I've run an event during the current month, I compare the figures and see if they're up, in which case, of course, I claim the credit—not a totally false claim.

At Rosewood, we don't run promotions just for the sake of running them. If the sales figures don't show a significant increase, and nothing untoward has happened, I take a strong look at either not repeating the same event or seeing how it can be improved.

Shirley gathered up the cheques and walked to the door. "You realize, of course, Jenny, that each one of them who brings up the rent will want a word with Bob or Keith or you."

"Yeah," I said, "and you know which one they'll most likely end up with. But they have to be dealt with sometime, so why not today? Try giving them the party line about 'not a random act', 'police investigation underway', etc. If that doesn't work, send them in here."

"Okay," she said.

"On second thought," I said, "buzz me and I'll come to the front. If they get one foot in here, I'll never get them out.

"Oh, yes—one last thing, Shirley, before I forget. Have some fresh flowers sent to the hospital for Mrs. Jones—first name Eulah. A large bouquet. Have the card read from the Management and Staff of Rosewood City Centre."

Eight

Our morning meeting never got off the ground. Keith had some sort of emergency in the electrical room that would likely tie him up for the rest of the morning, and Helen called to say she was at Police Headquarters at George's request and didn't know when she'd be in.

"Wonder what that's about? Can't be much new just since yesterday." Bob stood in the doorway of my office and looked around. "Nice to see you've cleared this place out a bit, Jenny." I guess he'd seen the pumpkins earlier. "I don't know how you stand being in here with all this stuff, let alone keep track of what it's all for."

"It's not hard, Bob." I put down my pen and leaned back in the chair, pointing around the room. "If it's a rabbit or a mushroom, it's for Easter; if it's a scarecrow, that's Thanksgiving; the blue light on the metal post with wheels flashes when you turn it on—that's for Sidewalk Sale Specials; the foam core apples are from the Back To School promo, and everything that is red, white or green is Christmas stuff."

I was sorry the minute the last few words left my mouth. Of course, he picked up on it right away. "Don't forget, Jenny, two o'clock sharp."

"I'm on it, Bob." I slid one hand under the desk and crossed my fingers. "But you know, Christmas is well in hand, and I'm totally ready for the Thursday board meeting. Later today, I'll get the boardroom set up. But d'you really think they're going to spend much time discussing Santa and company anyway?

"I think the best plan is to cover off the Christmas presentation quickly," I continued, "and go straight to the real agenda, which I'm sure will be the shootings and what we're gonna do to keep the shoppers coming. I've been thinking about that all weekend and can't say I've got any immediate solution in mind. Do we throw money at the problem? Take out more ads? Do nothing and hope for the best? There's bound to be some big time screaming for some kind of action from my department, Bob, and it seems to me that the sooner we can show them a plan, any plan, the better."

Bob looked at me for a long moment. "You're right," He hesitated a bit, leaned backwards out the door and looked up the hall towards the reception area. We'd both heard the door opening. "Let's spend a few minutes now on Christmas, and depending on how it sits, that'll be the end of it, and we can take the time this afternoon for the other."

He's like a dog with a bone, I thought. May as well just get to it.

The intercom buzzed as I went to the file cabinet to get out my Christmas promo folders. Bob picked it up and listened. After a couple of seconds, his eyebrows went up. "Indeed," he said. He listened for another few seconds. "Is that right?" he said. The eyebrows stayed up, a lot of emotion from Bob. "We'll see about that," he said. "Put them in my office."

He hung up, quietly but firmly, and stood, fastening his jacket. He pulled each shirt cuff down until exactly three-quarters of an inch of white showed below the sleeve. "Seems I have a delegation. We'll talk later."

I gave him time to get up the hall and into his office then

hurried along to Shirley's desk. She put a finger to her lips.

"What's going on?" I mouthed quietly. "What delegation?"

"Ssh, he'll hear you. I left the door open a bit so we could eavesdrop."

"Who's in there?" I sidled around on tiptoe to the wall behind her. She rolled her chair back closer to me and put her hand over her mouth, whispering in my ear. High intrigue, this.

"The first contingent of the morning, although I'm sure there's going to be a lot more. Seven of the independents arrived while Bob was in your office. Demanded to see him. They're not going to pay any rent until this murder business is solved. That's a direct quote from their spokesman, the guy from Leather & Stuff."

We cocked our heads towards the door but couldn't hear as well as we would have liked, so Shirley took a ruler off her desk, hitched up her skirt and got down on her knees. Quiet as a mouse, she slid the ruler forward along the floor until it caught the end of the door and nudged it open a couple more inches. She grinned up at me. "Works like a charm," she whispered.

A girl after my own heart, this one.

"Wheest," I whispered back. "Let's listen."

"…and so we're entitled to a rent abatement, and you may as well give us one, seein' as we're not gonna pay any rent anyway." That was Santillo from the Leather store. There was a lot of muttering and harrumphing and that's righting when he finished.

"Gentlemen, I appreciate your concern," Bob's voice was tight but smooth. "But before we discuss the rent issue, let me appraise you of the current situation.

"Inspector Anderson of the police department is positive this shooting is not a random act of violence. He does not feel that someone is targeting our customers, and he is holding a press conference this morning to that effect. In fact, our Security Chief, Ms. Lemieux, is with him as we speak.

"And right at this moment, our Promotion Director, Ms. Turnbull, is in her office mounting a comprehensive campaign to ensure we do not suffer a loss of customers…"

Shirley nodded firmly.

"…and I, myself, have meetings lined up with the Mayor, our own Head Office people and Mr. Jim Masters, publisher of the *Weekly Times*."

That one should be interesting, I thought.

"We are well aware of the seriousness of the situation, gentlemen, and are taking all possible measures to deal with it. And now, let me address your earlier collective statement."

Shirley and I inched a bit closer to the door. This was going to be good. Telling Bob that you won't pay the rent has the same result as throwing red meat to a shark.

"I will make this as succinct as possible," Bob said. "There will be no rent abatement, and you will pay your rent. Furthermore, as this is the first working day of the month, you will pay it before the end of office hours today. Refusing to pay is not an option. For those of you who do not agree, I suggest you read your lease thoroughly. If you still decide to withhold monies, you will be locked out. I shall instruct the bailiff to padlock your premises, and I shall then distrain your goods against monies owing. Re-entry will only be permitted on the full payment of all rent—which will, of course, include any outstanding promotional dues or other arrears—by cash or certified cheque. Do not mistake this as a threat, gentlemen, it is simply a statement of management policy. A policy that I endorse and will enforce fully under the terms of our lease agreement.

"And now, if you will excuse me…"

The only sound was Bob's chair being pushed back. Shirley and I moved like greased lightning, she to her desk and me down the hall to my office.

•

Bob left for Head Office straight after his meeting with the tenants, so I got my second reprieve of the morning—at least as far as Santa was concerned.

By lunchtime, I had met with at least another couple of dozen retailers, all with the same concerns. My standard patter was a public relations version of Bob's speech. I mean, what else could I add that would top what he'd said? The only difference was I tried to couch the same information in kinder terms.

It's always our aim to have at least one person on the management staff that the tenants aren't angry with at any given time, so I went for the "we're a team so let's work together and present a united front" approach. It worked for a number of them, mostly the experienced merchants, and I simply told the others to come back when Bob was here.

After the first six or so trips back and forth along the hall to talk to them, I gave up trying to get any work done and settled on the couch opposite Shirley.

"Keep your ear to the ground often, do you?" I asked her.

"How else can I steer this old boat?" she laughed. "Any secretary worth her salt has to keep up, Jenny."

"Thank God he didn't catch us," I said, "specially when you were rooting around on the floor."

"No problem." She tapped an eyelid. "Contact lenses are always a good excuse." Flipping a switch on the phone console, she got her purse out of a drawer. "I'm goin' down to pick up a sandwich for lunch. The Info Booth'll pick up the phones.

Can I get you one?"

"A toasted egg salad would be great, thanks. I'll get the tea ready. You sure you want to run the gamut, though? One step into the mall, and they'll be after you."

"No, they won't. I'm just the secretary."

•

After lunch, I pulled the Santa file from the stack of Christmas stuff on my desk, stuck it in the file cabinet behind the January Sidewalk Sale folders and scooped up the rest, including the video of last year's parade.

"Shirley, I'll be in the boardroom for a while. Keith's back now, so let him handle the afternoon shift. I'm all talked out.

"And, by the way, don't bother calling around about the funeral arrangements. I was speaking to Helen a few minutes ago. She's still at the cop shop, and apparently the bodies won't be released for another few days. They both have to be autopsied, and nobody seems to know when that's scheduled, so just let it go for now. But do make sure the flowers go to the hospital. Thanks."

The next hour flew past. I got everything that had anything to do with the Santa Parade spread out on the boardroom table and checked to see that all the i's were dotted and the t's crossed, pinned up the route map showing where the parade would march through the mall and put a copy of our new radio commercial in the tape player. A couple of easels holding four by five foot foam core blowups of our print ads and mall signs went up next. A copy of the Christmas budget went on the table for each of the Directors, and I added a candy cane to the top of each one.

I stood back and took a look around. Seemed fine to me.

I had originally intended to run the video of last year's parade at the meeting, but after thinking about it for two or three seconds, put it in my purse instead. No point in showing them Santa in all his glory.

The door opened, and Keith's head appeared. "Jenny, Bob phoned. He won't be back."

"Ever?" I asked, but the door closed, and he was gone.

Shirley buzzed through to say there was a fresh group of tenants waiting to see somebody from management.

"I can't, Shirl." I picked up my purse. "I'm gone for the day. Give them to Keith. He'll make short work of it."

Nine

The escalator handrail was smooth and clear of stickers. Tiny stepped off the bottom just as I started down. Watching him walk away, I felt the same little jolt of recognition. There was something about that gait.

"Yo, Tiny," I called. "Wait up."

He kept walking.

"Tiny," I jumped the last step and hurried after him. "Hold on a minute."

He sped up.

I stopped and watched him. For a fat man, he sure was zippin' right along. So much for trying to be friendly to a new staff member. I walked across the centre court to the Info Booth and signed out.

"I'm leaving for today, Mare. See you tomorrow."

A quick pass through the wool store found a girl who was filling in temporarily and who knew nothing about new wool, new suppliers or local sheep farmers.

I'd never been in the store without Cathy there, and most times, she'd had a group of beginner knitters sitting at a table at the back. They'd always looked so cozy, and the table was invariably heaped with practice pieces of knitting lying around between styrofoam cups, a teapot and an assortment of baked goods—it made me feel right at home, and I'd joined them for a quick cuppa on more than one occasion.

Why do nice people have to die before their time? I was sure gonna miss Cathy, and the thought that this girl might end up running the store made me shudder. Her main interest seemed to be a small hangnail on one of her fingers. She did promise, however, to ask Mr. Haggerty when he came in later to close up.

"You won't forget now, will you?" I asked. "It's really important."

"I won't forget," she said. "Give me your phone number, and I'll call you tomorrow, first thing."

"Just call up to the management office, they'll find me. I'm the Promotion Director."

"What's a Promotion Director?"

She held a pencil ready. Maybe she was going to write down the answer.

"Don't worry about it. Just ask for Jenny."

•

"I got your message," Helen said. "Loud and clear." She came down the stairs into the kitchen. "What are we having and when do we eat?"

"Chicken and biscuits." I opened the oven door and set the little circles of dough down gently in the bubbling casserole. "Gravy, mashed potatoes and brussels sprouts. Ten minutes. Pour yourself a glass of wine for now. It's in the fridge."

"Boy," she said, "even the table's set. Must've been some day."

Before starting up the Chevy, I'd concentrated hard on Helen. "Please come home. Food's ready. Please come home.' Then I'd driven to our favourite butcher's for some free-range chicken breasts, stopped at the market and loaded up with organically-grown veggies and finished up at the wine store, keeping up my chant the whole time.

"Some few days, you mean, don't you?" I took the pressure cooker off the stove and over to the sink to run it under the cold tap. The little widgetty-waw on top bobbed back and forth, sending spurts of steam flying.

"For Pete's sake, Jenny, that thing's a bomb." Helen's always hated the pressure cooker. She used to leave the room the minute she saw me get it out. Now she just stays over by the door and hangs on to the knob. Progress of a sort, I guess.

"Safe as houses." I unclamped the lid and drained the spuds. "My mother used one for forty years, and she only had it blow once."

I threw in a lump of butter, some milk and grated cheese and started mashing.

"Oh, well then." Cocky now that the lid was off and we weren't riding the sky train, she let go of her anchor and sauntered back to the table. "So what's all this in aid of, White Man? Not that I'm complaining, mind you. I had dinner with George last night. Pizza at the cop shop. It was pretty disgusting, and by the time he'd finished with phone calls, faxes and people running in and out of his office, it was cold to boot."

"It's a little regroup session." I put the food on the table and sat down. "I need to talk to a real person. But dig in first, and let's eat."

There was a couple of minutes silence while we loaded up our plates and got started.

"God, this is good," Helen helped herself to more sprouts. "Bet you got these at that organic place. Wonder what our tenants would think if they found out we don't shop at the mall."

"Fuck the tenants and their sales figures and their rent

problems." I spooned a little more gravy over my potatoes. "The same can go for over-sensitive publishers, over-bearing politicians and overweight maintenance people. And don't forget those poor little sales people with hangnails. The ones who wouldn't recognize an original thought if it fuckin' bit them."

Helen got up and put the kettle on. "Y'know, Jenny," she said, "I wish you'd work on getting over this shyness of yours. Learn to speak right up."

She opened the china cabinet and got out cups and saucers—the Royal Albert ones, no less. This girl knew, all right.

"I'll make us a pot of tea. You stab a few more biscuits or sprouts or something."

After dinner, settled by the fire with a tea-tray, I unloaded everything while Helen just sat and nodded, shook her head and other than chuckling a bit here and there, generally kept quiet until I ran out of steam.

"What bothered you the most?" she asked when I'd finished. "Three men turning their back on you? Finding a body? Or somebody not knowing what you do for a living? I mean, how awful can it be? With the exception of Jim, which of the others means anything? I bet if you made up a list of who's important in your life, the only one who'd make it would be Jim, and after the liver stuff, even he'd be hanging on by his fingernails. In fact, I think he was hanging there already."

She got up and refilled the kettle. "And as for the tenants, Jenny, you should be used to them by now. You know they all go to the same school. And you know damn well if you live in the swamp, you gotta deal with the alligators. Besides, they're not all awful. You really liked Cathy Haggerty, didn't you?"

"Yeah, and look what happened to her." I wasn't quite ready to hang it up yet. "You know, Helen, if you weren't working there too, I'd quit."

Her dark eyes locked on my face for a long minute. "No, you wouldn't, Jenny. You love that job, and you know it. Now why don't you just spit out what's really bothering you, and let's get to it?"

"Santa."

"I thought so."

"It's not so much Bob and the board meeting I'm worried about. God knows I've pulled the wool over their collective eyes on more than one occasion, and they can't take you out and shoot you just because a promotion goes wrong. No. It's the customers. I've always prided myself on Rosewood having the single best mall Christmas anywhere. We've got people who come, year after year, from miles around, just because they know the decorations and the Santa parade and setup will be bigger and better every time.

"Then there's all the parents who bring their kids for the picture-taking with good old St. Nick. It's a big thing for them. A lot of those pictures get sent overseas to grandparents. One mother told me last year she can't afford a camera or studio pictures, so she sends one of our three-dollar photos to her parents in Italy every year so they can see how big the kids are getting."

I got up and started pacing. "I can't let them down, Helen. I can't and I won't."

Helen turned sideways in her chair and watched me. Her head was going from side to side like a tennis fan, and she was smiling.

"What?" I asked.

"You're pacing," she said. "That's a good sign. Means something's gonna get done."

"Damn straight, it is. Even if it means I have to put on that red velvet outfit myself."

"Now there's a thought." She stood up and lifted the tray. "How about we get these dishes done, now that you're sorta back on track?"

"Just leave them. I can't be worrying about a few plates. I'll throw them out and buy new ones. Pots, too. Right now, I've got to think."

"Okay," she said and started up the stairs. "I'm for a bath, a bit of reading and then bed. Thanks for dinner, Jen. It was wonderful."

"Helen?"
"What?"
"Thank you."
"Any time."

Ten

Another fifteen minutes of pacing and thinking and thinking and pacing produced nothing in the way of where to find a replacement Santa. For the umpteenth time I said to myself, there really ought to be a Santa school that a person could just phone and have one sent over.

A few times over the years, the idea's been put forward, but nobody's ever got around to starting one. There's probably money in it somewhere. Just look what I would pay right about now for a good Father Christmas.

The operative word here is "good". It's not easy being Santa. First and foremost, he has to like kids or at least have the patience of Job. The babies either spit up or pee all over him. The one to five-year-olds bawl or kick him in the shins, and the six-to-ten age group can never sit still long enough because they don't want to be there in the first place, so they usually get even by sticking out their tongue just as the camera clicks. Of course, then the parent-in-charge doesn't like the picture, and you have to take another one or two or three.

When you, the promotion director, are lucky enough to find a person who can handle all that, you now get to tell him that you're going to stuff him into a red velvet and white fur suit that weighs a ton and'll make him sweat like a horse. Of course, you don't tell him the last part; he finds that out in the first half-hour.

Speaking of hours—that's next. Santa, this paragon of virtue, has to arrive early, stay late and do a few walk-abouts between picture-taking hours. He has to shake hands, smile a lot and constantly be saying "HO, HO, HO!" He can't be seen eating, drinking and smoking in public or using a public washroom and, of course, crumbs or soup dribbles on his beard and stains on his suit are major no-nos. So is any form of retaliation against the shin-kickers.

The biggest difficulty in finding such a gem is that most of the men who could fit even half of the criteria are working in some great-paying full-time job somewhere, and you can only offer a six-week engagement, albeit at double or triple a normal working wage. Actors between jobs can be a great source, but you have to take a chance, because if a gig comes up, they're gone!

Just like my Santa—gone!

I went into the bedroom and hauled out my overflow carton from under the bed. It's full of notes on empty matchbook covers and scribbles on bits torn from cigarette packages along with scraps of paper holding those brilliant ideas that come to me just before falling asleep. Somewhere in there, I reasoned, might be a contact for a Santa. I had a vague recollection of a couple of names of seniors who might do in a pinch.

Anyway, I love an excuse to go through the box. It's like a little personal archaeological dig, sifting through layers, each one to its own season. Now if I could just find July. That's when I would've been working on the Santa bit.

July was there all right, but the names weren't. I must have thrown them away when I'd made the deal with Doug White, the quitter. I mentally changed his name forever to Black. Black as the Earl O'Hell's waistcoat as far as I was concerned.

Only other thing I can do, I thought, is phone a couple of

my promotion buddies at other shopping centres. Maybe one of them can help me out.

I figured that since I was that far into it, it seemed as good a time as any to go over the video of last year's parade for a final spot check. I went through to the other room, made a fresh cuppa and sat down to watch it.

The pipers burst onto the screen first. God love those guys. Not only do they give a rousing start to any parade, but they're better than horses at parting a crowd. There's something about thirty-some large men in kilts marching to the skirl of pipes, especially in an enclosed space, that makes people stand back. I like it, of course. For me, it's mother's milk, but I can appreciate that others find it a bit awesome.

Next came an assortment of majorettes, all sizes in all ages, followed by a few local minor sports teams in uniform. Rosewood Centre, good citizen that it is, sponsors a team each in baseball, hockey and lacrosse, and they were always up for a good parade. After the majorettes came the service clubs, some forty-strong decked out in full regalia. Man, that's a powerful sight. Almost, but not quite, competition for the pipers.

In addition to all this glory, there were a dozen or so elves and clowns skipping about, handing out candy canes. Every year I give them all a big lecture about how they're supposed to stay on the outside edge and try to form some sort of barrier to keep the crowd from joining the marchers. It never works, except in theory. On the big day, everybody forgets whatever they've been told and gets swept up in the moment. It's at this point that our security staff are needed to poke them back into place and keep things together.

Last year's video looked pretty good. The cameraman had done a good job of following the action. I hit the pause button just as Santa reached his castle. This was my favourite bit, and

I wanted to savour it for a few minutes. Every year we set aside a particular area for the children and staff of a "special needs" home in our neighbourhood. Most of the kids were in wheelchairs, some wore leg or backbraces and others were mentally challenged. But all of them knew Santa.

When he got down off his sleigh and entered their special spot, the looks on their faces made everything worth it. Each of the men I'd hired to fill the job said afterwards that this part of the job was what they always took away with them. In fact, I've never seen one Santa come out of that area with dry eyes, and every time I watch the video from the previous year, I have a little cry myself and promise to try and be a better person.

I hit the start button and watched again as Santa spent a few minutes with each of them. Giving the last two a big hug, he turned and walked towards his outsize chair to take up residence for the next six weeks.

And there it was. Simple as that.

Eleven

Next morning, I hummed the "Hallelujah Chorus" all the way to work, scarcely able to believe my good fortune. Roll on ten o'clock. All I had to do was to convince Tiny that it was his good fortune too. I could just tell him he was going to be wearing different coveralls for a while but, being a diplomatic sort of girl and remembering how he'd scuttled across the mall when he'd heard my voice yesterday, I decided it might be prudent to use a bit of finesse.

The only damper on the morning's drive was the number of large, fluffy snowflakes coming down, the kind that stayed on the ground. I automatically thought of having to bank the Chevy soon and get out my little winter runabout. I also had to get to that wool farm before the weather socked in. Two hours or so driving through snow wasn't my idea of a good time. If Hangnail Hannah from the wool store had the address, maybe I could wangle a day at the end of the week to get up there. I could make it the last spin for the Chevy that winter and kill two birds with one stone.

When I got up to the office, Shirley was already at her desk with her first cup of coffee. Double cream, three sugars. No wonder she couldn't sit still for long.

"Morning, Shirl. Isn't it a wonderful day?"

"You must've found a Santa."

That stopped me on the spot.

"How in the name of the Wee Man, Shirley, did you know I'd even lost one?"

She chuckled and tapped her right eyelid. "The all-seeing eye. Remember?"

"Shirley, tell me you haven't been crawling around the floor outside my office. Isn't the hallway a bit risky, even for the contact lens story?"

She ignored that and followed me into the kitchen to read out my messages, while I filled the kettle and plugged it in.

"Detective Hobart, re a Mr. Dick Simmons. A Mr. Dick Simmons, re a lawsuit. Now that one was ugly. Matthew Leung, re the Thursday meeting. Barb Donaldson, from the paper—something about a great plan she's got for extra advertising 'cause of the murders."

"I'll bet," I muttered.

"Jim Masters—didn't say what it's about." She shuffled through some more pink slips. "Oh yes, there was a note on my desk when I came in that said—quote, Tiny can't come up at ten…he's got to paint the curbs, unquote."

"That it?"

"Yep. Except one from Mary at Info. There's an address down at the booth somebody left for you last night. Want me to phone down for it?"

"No, thanks. I'll pick it up. I have to go down and see Ed, anyway."

I unplugged the kettle. "Just give me twenty minutes or so and then put this back on, will you? And while you're at it, ask Helen, when you see her, if she's got time to have a bite of lunch? I want to catch up on what's what with the police investigation."

•

"You want what?" Ed's voice went up a couple of notches.

We were sitting on a mall bench outside the coffee bar. Ed was downing a jumbo, black, and it was obvious he wasn't as thrilled about my brainwave as I was.

"But, Ed," I got the words out fast, "he's perfect. Absolutely perfect."

"But…"

"And I'm stuck, Ed. Really stuck. I could lose my job over this. Tiny is my only out. Please, Ed."

"But…"

"Think of the money. I'll double what you're paying him, and he'll still be on your payroll as well till I'm finished with him, and besides, I only need him for six measly weeks. That's all, six little weeks. They'll fly past, you'll see."

"Well, I'm sure he could use the extra cash. What with his father and all."

He was weakening. I had him. Thank you, Jesus.

"And tell you what… I'll get my boys in here after school every day this week. All of 'em. They'll help Tiny paint the curbs. My cost. The job'll be done before you know it."

He chucked his empty coffee cup in the garbage bin next to us and stood up. "You win. As usual. But only on one condition."

"Name it."

"You get Tiny's agreement to do this. I'm not ordering it up. I'll have enough trouble explaining to Keith, let alone Mr. Graham, why I'm paying someone who's not on the job."

"No problem. Just leave it to me. I'll talk to Tiny and explain things to Keith. But we'll have to keep it from Bob till at least after the parade. And don't forget now, you'll have access to any of my kids when you need them, so you won't really be short-handed, will you?"

"I'm going now, before you think of something else."
I gave him a quick hug. "Thanks, Ed. You're a doll."

•

The wool farm address was printed in large childlike letters on the back of a yarn label. Written across the top was "to the promotion person" with a question mark. I picked up a walkie-talkie at the booth and called upstairs.

"I'm gonna do a walkabout while I'm down here, Shirl. I'll keep the radio with me in case you need me for anything."

The shopping centre looked pretty normal. All the tenants were open and ready for business, and even though it was still quite early, there were quite a number of customers. My usual tour, which I try to do at least three times a day, takes me around both levels, sitting at various vantage points in the mall. I have a mental check list of things to look for, depending on what time of day I'm sitting there and what day of the week it is. Like most other businesses, the shopping centre industry has its own habits and peculiarities, and I believe the biggest part of my job is knowing what those are.

There are all sorts of companies which specialize in trying to sell you an expensive study of area "demographics"—a word I absolutely hate—along with "target market customer", "traffic patterns", "income levels", etc.

Most research studies can be made to read whatever you want them to read but, in my book, if you want to find out who your customers really are, sit in the mall. If you want to know where they shop, look at what they're carrying. After all, would you run a fashion show if the majority of your customers were in pink sponge rollers with husbands in baseball caps and carrying bags from a discount store?

If you want to know the average income level in the area, drive around the neighbourhood. Look at the average home and what kind of car is parked in the driveway.

For a customer count of your quietest or busiest days and times, check out the parking lot. At a couple of predetermined times, drive around and count the empty spaces, then subtract that from the number of parking stalls you've got, figuring an average of two people per car.

And there you have it. All the data you need, it doesn't cost a cent and you can impress the hell out of the Board of Directors, especially when you're trying to go for an increase in the budget. At the very least, they'll know you did your homework.

Our tenant mix serves a population that is somewhat middle-to-high income with a matching intelligence level, lots of kids and a healthy smattering of ethnic groups. Our leasing people also set aside a couple of large premises for discount stores recently but, so far, only one is occupied, and it doesn't do too badly. You can tell a lot about the current state of the economy, national and local, by watching the monthly sales figures, and up to the last weekend's little fiasco, ours had been pretty good.

•

Thoughts of the shooting got me upstairs and into my office to return Detective Hobart's call. I punched the buttons with my fingers crossed but didn't really think he'd called to tell me Simmons was the shooter. Much as I loved the thought of him being arrested, it seemed too good to be true.

"Hobart speaking." The voice was gruff and sounded tired.

"Good morning, Detective. Jenny Turnbull returning your call."

"Oh, yeah, the shopping centre."

Pause. I waited. Nothing. "What can I do for you, Detective?" Still nothing. I thought Helen said these guys were good. "Detective?"

"Yeah…sorry," He cleared his throat. "Just looking for my notes. Hang on a minute."

The phone clunked down on the desk, and there were another few moments of silence, broken by the sound of paper rustling, before he picked it back up.

"Inspector Anderson asked me to give you a call. Thought you'd want to know. Dick Simmons is clear. Bartolo and I interviewed him on Sunday, and his story checks out. He's not your shooter."

"What is his story, Detective?"

"Seems he was sitting outside the shoe repair store waving a hand-made sign saying 'Don't bring your shoes here or you'll be sorry' at the time of the shooting. The shoe repair guy confirms it. He put a call into your Security to get him moved, but I guess with all the excitement over the shots going off and everything else, they didn't get down there and forgot to make a written report."

"I can certainly believe that," I said. "Oh, well. I was hoping."

"Don't know as I blame you. He's certainly one plug-ugly customer, that one. Nice wife, though. Funny how that happens, isn't it? Anyway, when we left, he was on the phone to a lawyer and shouting about a lawsuit. That's why Inspector Anderson wanted me to give you a heads up. We're sure you're gonna hear from him soon."

"Already have. Anyway, thank you for letting me know, Detective. I appreciate it. Anything else happening with the investigation I should know about?"

"I'm not at liberty to talk about an ongoing investigation, ma'am, but I'm sure Inspector Anderson will be in touch with your management sometime today for an update. He always makes it a point to do that." He made a low sound, kind of like a mixture of a chuckle and a cough. "And, of course, there's always Ms. Lemieux."

I almost heard him wink at the phone. "Exactly." I could like this guy. "Anyway, thanks again. And the next time you and Detective Bartolo find yourselves over this way, come up to the office. Maybe we can have some lunch or something."

"We'll do that, Miss Turnbull."

"Jenny, please."

"Okay. See ya."

I buzzed through to Shirley. "If Dick Simmons calls again, I'm not available. If he's threatening a lawsuit, I'm not going to get involved in all that bullshit. It's gonna end up with Bob and our legal department, anyway, so you may as well give it to him in the first place. But warn him about it first, will you? And tell him it's confirmed that Simmons is not the shooter."

"Too bad, eh, Jenny?"

"Sure is, but what can you do? By the way, did you get those flowers sent to the hospital yesterday?"

"Yep. And I've got the funeral arrangements here for Cathy Haggerty and Gerry Menard, soon as the bodies are released. I'll leave a copy on your desk later."

I dialled the *Weekly Times*.

"This is Barb Donaldson speaking."

"Hi, Barb. This is Jenny Turnbull from Rosewood City Centre returning your call. What can I do for you this fine morning?"

"Boy, you sure sound chipper. Somebody catch your murderer?"

"Was there something you wanted?"

"I'm just on my way over to see you." She sounded delighted at the prospect. That made one of us. "I've come up with a couple of great ideas about getting your customers back. Some promotions and some extra advertising. Stuff like that."

Now that was really professional— "stuff like that"? This babe was definitely not going to last—at least not as my advertising guru.

"Sorry, Babs…"

"It's Barb," she cut in.

"…no can do. Certainly not this afternoon. As a matter of fact, the rest of the week's out, too. Besides, as you know, our Christmas advertising is all in place."

"But, what about the shootings? What about the retailers? What about their lost sales?"

"What about them?" I asked.

"That's what I need to talk to you about. My ideas. I can be there in five minutes."

"We seem to have a tiny breakdown in communication here. Let me try again. I can't see you this afternoon. In fact, I can't see you this week. To answer your other questions, the police are handling the shootings, the retailers are all open for business, and their sales are quite normal. But thank you for asking. As for extra advertising or new ideas, Rosewood won't be doing anything that will necessitate your input for the rest of the season. Except, of course, to monitor that our bookings run as scheduled. I'll call you in early December to arrange our January Sidewalk Sale Advertising. We'll have a little Christmas lunch."

"Well, if you're sure." She didn't sound quite so delighted now. "I guess I can't force you to see me, but I'm sure Mr. Masters will be calling you."

"I'm sure he will. In the meantime, Barb, you have the best day you can, and I'll talk to you next month."

I put the phone down gently in the cradle. One part of me felt kind of sorry for Babs, having once been an advertising sales rep myself. I knew how they're pushed to constantly produce lineage, especially on a weekly paper. And nearly every paper I knew paid by commission with a base salary that barely ranked at starvation level.

However, as my mother would say, "you catch more flies with honey than vinegar", and Ms. Donaldson's last words had sounded like a threat to me.

The intercom buzzed. "Matthew Leung on the line."

"Mr. Leung, how are you? You were next on my list of calls. What can I do for you?"

"Good morning, Miss Turnbull." His voice was cultured, and he was very soft-spoken. No slang from Mr. Leung.

Small, tidy and sharp as a pencil, he'd been President of the Merchants' Association for two years in a row, a thankless job which he carried out with panache. He was highly professional, willing to consider all proposals and even willing to take on any tenants he felt were not pulling their share in the centre advertising and special events.

He was a gem to work with, but there was a sidebar to it. Whenever I was trying to slightly fudge a proposal to the board, I always felt he would be the one to spot it. So far, I'd gotten away with most of the minor things, but there was always that edge, and I prefer to have the edge on my side.

"I apologize for calling a second time, but I must insist on speaking with you this morning. A problem has come up."

"Something I can help with, Mr. Leung?"

"A family matter. But thank you. I am unable to attend the Thursday meeting. It is necessary that I travel to Hong Kong today."

"Oh, dear."

"I'm afraid so. But I have prepared some material for the meeting. Perhaps you will do me the service of presenting it."

"Of course. I'm sorry you won't be there, but if you leave the papers in your store, I'll stop by this afternoon and pick them up."

"That is of great assistance. Thank you." His phone made no sound as he hung up.

I kicked off my shoes, shoved the chair back and swung my feet up on the desk. One more problem had just removed itself. Was this a great day or what?

When I get to rule the world, I'm going to arrange for everybody to have a day like this at least five times a week.

•

"Well, Paleface, you're certainly in a good mood. I could hear the humming at the end of the corridor. What's goin' on?"

Helen stood in the doorway, loaded up with deli packages.

"Come in, come in." I swiped at the desk to clear off the middle. "You didn't have to bring lunch. I was gonna treat, but seeing as it's here, let's eat."

"Think maybe you could put your feet down first?"

She spread out slices of cold turkey breast and a couple of containers with warm German potato salad and coleslaw. Another bag produced slices of dark rye bread, two bottles of spring water and an apple each. She finished up by setting a bottle of Dijon mustard in the middle.

"I know you prefer ballpark mustard, Jenny, but I can't stand the stuff, so you'll just have to put up with the real thing."

A quick fish around her blazer pockets produced an assortment of plastic knives, forks and spoons along with a bunch of paper serviettes. We set to, loading up our plates.

"Helen, I owe you an apology for last night."

"What are you apologizing for?"

"I was thinking on the way in this morning that I hadn't even asked you how your last couple of days were. I know you've been spending a lot of time over at the cop shop. And somehow I can't believe it's all because of George."

"Well, I'd be lying if I said I don't still enjoy being around him, but there's no way I'd ever go back to what I left." She stopped eating and looked across the desk at me. "You know better than anyone how hard I worked at getting over that situation."

Both of us were quiet for a few minutes. Then she gave herself a little shake and picked up her fork.

"No." Her voice was decisive as only Helen's can be. "If George and I do anything at all about the situation, I'll make sure it's only on a one-night stand basis."

I grinned at her. "I'm shocked."

"What, you want I should scream over something I gave up willingly years ago? Get real."

We ate in silence for a bit, both of us, no doubt, thinking about George, but from two different perspectives. Helen was certainly a big girl, but she was also my best friend, and the last thing I wanted was for her to get hurt. I wondered silently if there was anything I could do about the situation.

"Forget it, Jenny. I know what you're thinking, and it's no go. You'd be better off concentrating on what you're going to do about your own love life. From the little you said about your dinner date the other night, it's not in very good shape."

"And whose fault is that?" Her eyebrows went up. "Maybe I did overreact a little, but he didn't have to walk away and leave me standing there like a knotless thread."

I picked up the plates and sundries and stacked them for recycling later.

"Let's get back to the subject at hand. What about the murders? Surely George's people have to be getting somewhere."

"Well," she said, "we can forget about the pirate thing. The hook belonged to the cook at Capt'n Billy's Fish and Chips. All his people were dressed in costumes, and he saw the door open when he was in the hall putting out garbage, so he pulled it shut to stop kids from running in the back hallway. The woman who said she saw the hook was just confused about the time. Turns out she saw it long before the shootings."

I scraped up the last bits of the potato salad from the tub while she polished an apple on her lapel.

"The investigation seems to be centering around Menard," she said. "It looks like there might be more than simply a social connection between him and Jones Jr."

"Is that right?" I asked. "Like what?"

"That's what George's people are trying to put together. Some of his guys on the beat are hearing talk of everything from drugs to gay bashing…"

"Bit strong for gay bashing, isn't it?" I interrupted.

"…to that teen prostitution business Menard's buddy was running. When they had the van at the back of the parking lot to service the shopping public."

"God, Helen, can you just imagine Jones Sr. if it turns out his son was involved in that? I'm beginning to feel more sorry than ever for the mother."

I cleared up the desk while she finished her last bit of apple.

"Me, too." She slam-dunked the apple core into the wastebasket and wiped her hands. "Trouble is, nobody'll say anything concrete, so everything's still too vague to nail down, but a pattern is definitely forming. George has got a couple of detectives helping Hobart and Bartolo, doing the rounds of Menard and Jones' favourite haunts. Why are you nodding, Jenny?"

"I'm not surprised," I said. "Because of my knitting, you see."

"No, I don't see. What's your knitting got to do with anything?"

"Simple," I said. "Any knitter knows that everything conforms to a pattern. It might look difficult when you first start, but once you figure out the pattern, it all comes together. That's all."

Helen stood up and wiped a few stray crumbs off her lap. "I'll be sure to tell that to George. I'm sure he'll appreciate the insight."

"Don't go yet, Hel. Sit down. What's happening about bodies? Surely they've finished the autopsies by now? And what about Jones Jr.? He still alive? C'mon, sit and spill."

"I can't. I've got a staff to see to." She stayed on her feet. "The bodies are getting released tomorrow. The autopsies are done. I hope to get to read the reports later on this aft and yes, Jones Jr. is still alive. Barely, mind you, but alive. Although, if the cops find any connection between him and Menard, his father'll probably do him in. Don't forget, His Councillorship has a reputation to uphold in the community."

"God, what a pair they are," I said. "Wonder what the wife's like?"

"She's got to be either just like them or a saint, I should think," Helen said. "I met her once at a luncheon for something or other. George introduced us, but it was brief, and she was half-hidden by her husband, so I didn't really talk to her. Small woman, thin and sorta beige-looking. Pleasant enough, but overshadowed by Jones. Too bad you didn't get in to see her on Sunday."

"I'm going tonight." I said.

"What about Jones?"

"There's a Council meeting at City Hall. About the new property tax structure. He proposed it, so he'll have to be there."

"Okay, I'm off then. See you later."

"Probably. By the way, I'm taking Saturday off. Going to take a drive to that sheep farm. Last spin for the Chevy before the weather socks in. Want to come?"

"No thanks," she chuckled. "My Cree ancestors were hunters, not farmers, so if I saw a sheep, I might have to kill it."

She left to go back to her office. On her way down the hall, I heard her saying "hello" and Ed's voice answering with the question, "Jenny in her office?"

"In here," I called. "Come in and take a load off."

"I'm only staying a minute, Jenny," he sat down opposite me. "Came up to say I've changed my mind."

I shot to my feet. "You can't, Ed. You just can't. We had a deal. You simply cannot back out when we had a deal."

"Relax, Jenny. I'm not backing out."

"What then…?"

"I've changed my mind about you talking to Tiny. After we talked this morning, I got to thinking about your first meeting with him. Didn't go too well, as I recall, so I think it's better if I tell him about our arrangement. Sort of smooth things out a bit first, maybe. What d'you think?"

I sat back down. This was better than best. "Ed, will you marry me?"

"Sure. But first, I'll have to go home and kill my wife."

We looked at each other and laughed.

Twelve

After Ed left, I did a bit of paper work on next year's Mother's Day promotions. As usual, I was running a "My Mom's the Best" contest. In its fourth year, it had proven to be one of our most popular events.

Towards the end of the year, I send a letter to all the local grade schools asking the teachers to have the kids write me a letter telling why they think their mother is the best of the lot. The kids get large buttons with our logo and "My Mom's the Best" printed on them, and we display all the letters throughout the shopping centre, by school and grade. The idea is that the kids will insist their parents and grandparents come to read them.

A panel of volunteer merchants plus Helen and myself read all the letters and cull them, eventually coming up with three winners. These mothers get prizes that have been donated by merchants, and although the first year's gifts were a bit cheezy and had to be fleshed out by my promotion budget, we've had some excellent prizes handed over since then.

My original intention was to have one winning mom and make her "Queen of Rosewood" for a day, but the response was so overwhelming and the letters so sincere, that it was impossible to limit it to just one. So I dropped the "Queen" idea and now I just make a little ceremony in Centre Court for three mothers, some of the Board members and the local press.

A disappointing number of the letters each year say "my mom's the best 'cause she buys me this, that or the other…" which I find rather sad, but my all-time favourite—and first winning one—said "my mom's the best 'cause she loves me." I have that one framed on my office wall.

Picking up my change purse, I went up the hall.

"Shirley, see if you can find Keith for me, please. Ask him to meet me downstairs at the Bagel Bonanza. My treat."

She held out a sheet of paper as I went passed her desk. "Here's the scoop on the funerals for Gerry Menard and Cathy Haggerty," she said. "Want me to arrange flowers?"

"Yes, please. Send them to the funeral homes. Just have Rosewood City Centre put on the cards."

"The Haggerty family has asked for donations to the Cancer Society. Seems she had a bout with it last year."

"Send flowers anyway. I'll see to the donation. Thanks, Shirl."

•

"You're going to do what?" Keith was sounding a lot like Ed had sounded earlier. He took off his glasses and shook his head. "I don't think so. And what about Bob? Haven't you told him you've had a Santa since the summer? Situations like this drive him nuts. You know that."

"Now, Keith, don't snake me here. Just think it through. I was in the worst jam of my life…"

"For this month at least," he cut in.

"…and this is the perfect solution."

"How do you figure that?" He waved his hand at the waitress and pointed to his cup. She nodded and came over with the coffeepot.

"Hi, Jenny," she said. "Hear you found a great Santa this year."

"Paula, we've got the real Santa." I couldn't look at Keith. I could feel the heat from his scowl. "Wait till you see him." She went back over to the counter.

"Would that be the royal 'we'?" he asked.

"Look, Keith. You get five workers for the price of one. Your three miles of curbs get painted this week before the snow starts in earnest. Your payroll stays the same. Your guy gets triple wages…"

"…and you get what you want. Again."

"Keith, I'm wounded. It's not about what I want. It's about survival."

I looked down and spoke softly into my glass of apple juice. "What happened about our 'one hand washing the other' routine? You forgotten already about me moving up the boat and camping show last Spring 'cause you'd arranged to have the floors stripped that week and never told anybody? Cost me hundreds in cancelled advertising, that little exercise." I lifted my head and looked over his shoulder at Paula. How'd she find out so fast, anyway? "And what about the time the landscape people never showed up? Whose kids jumped in to help with that? And who didn't tell Bob any of it?"

Keith put his glasses back on and held up his hands. I stopped talking.

"You win, Jenny. As usual."

Ed's very words.

He started to slide out of the booth. I put my hand out and pinned his sleeve to the table.

"Just one more thing, Keith. A key element."

He didn't say a word. Just lifted his eyebrows.

"Not a word to Bob. I'll tell him after the parade."

He stood up and jerked his jacket away from my hand. "Thanks for the bagel. I think."

•

Back in my office, I read over the notes from Matthew Leung. They were mainly about the responses from the tenants he'd talked to about the shootings and a general summary from him. As expected, the biggest concern was loss of revenue if the murders seriously impacted our customer count, but on the whole, most of them had agreed not to knee-jerk. The two weeks after Halloween were always on a bit of a holding pattern before the Christmas season got cranked up, so sales were usually down a bit then, anyway. He also suggested that Mall Management—in the form of Bob—try to get weekly sales figures as a yardstick, and that I do a customer count at each entrance door during those hours that normally are considered the busiest. Good suggestions, both of them.

The customer count was easy. Just a matter of having a couple of my kids sit at the doors with those little hand-held clicker geegaws stores use for inventory counting. And I couldn't really see a problem with getting weekly sales figures, especially as the idea came from their duly elected Merchants Association President.

He ended with the opinion that if management kept in close contact with the police to monitor the situation and kept the merchants informed every step of the way, things could be quite well controlled. All in all, a pretty positive outlook—one I was sure Bob wouldn't mind taking into the meeting.

A glance up the hall showed Bob's office door closed and no Shirley at her desk. Grabbing a juice from the kitchen, I went back and stuck a "Do Not Knock or Enter" sign on my door, closed it after me and plucked my "To Do" list off the wall so I could scratch off the bit about panicking re S. The only thing I had to worry about now was finding out if the Santa suit would be big enough for Tiny. Didn't really matter. There was a week and a half left to get another couple made. No problem.

I was feeling quite smug, actually. Everything had panned out beautifully, and it had only cost me some extra hours for the boys. I patted myself on the back. Gotta like it, Jenny.

Another hour went to rescheduling the boys over the next week or so, phoning to confirm that Mrs. Jones was still in hospital—she was—and that the younger Jones was still breathing—he was—and that the Council meeting was still on for tonight—it was. Could it get any better?

I was feeling so good, it seemed like the perfect time to call Jim and try to get over Sunday's sour note. I had my hand on the phone just as the door opened and Bob came in, my sign in his hand. "Playing Greta Garbo this afternoon?"

"Bob." I left my hand where it was. "I was just about to call through to you. Got any time to go over the Christmas promotion? We really should get to it before Thursday, you know. And there's a report here from Matthew Leung you should take a look at. He had to leave for Hong Kong unexpectedly, so he's left his notes for us to take into the meeting. And I've got the details of the funerals here, so we have to decide which of us is going to which one. Or maybe we should all go to both. What d'you think?"

Bob sat down with a heavy sigh and put his feet up on the desk. Today's dress code called for dark-blue pin stripes, a whiter-than-white shirt and a mottled grey and red tie. *Très vogue*, but that was our Bob.

"Jenny, Jenny." He rubbed a hand over his eyes. "Don't

rattle on. It just makes me crazy when I'm not in the mood for it. Which, by the way, is now."

"But, Bob, you know we only have a couple of weeks till the parade, and you said you were anxious to go over things. I just thought…"

He put a hand out to stop me. "I'm well aware of what I said. But I've had two friggin' awful days. Between Head Office and and the Mayor and Jim Masters and his lousy friggin' newspaper, I'm worn out…" Strong language for Bob. "…and now Shirley tells me your friend, Dick Simmons, is screaming about suing us and the repair shop and anybody else he doesn't like, which seems to cover the whole friggin' town. Just what I need right now."

"What about Jim?" I asked.

"I might have known you'd pick that one first. What's that you're drinking?"

"Grapefruit juice. Want a mouthful?" I held out the glass.

"Maybe I could have a whole one of my own?"

I burst out laughing.

"What's so funny?"

He sounded so petulant, I couldn't help but laugh even harder. "When we were kids and told to set the table for tea, my sister and I would put out milk and sugar and four cups and saucers, but, for some reason, we only ever put out one teaspoon." Off I went again. I could hardly speak for laughing. Even Bob was starting to grin. "Anyway, it became a family joke, and my father used to sigh and say 'if only I could have a spoon of my own'." I got up and went around the desk, patting his feet as I passed him. "I'll get you a juice, and then we'll talk."

He looked at his watch. "I've got a better idea, why don't I buy you dinner? I've got to stick around for a few hours anyway and catch up on some paper work. All this business has really put me behind. I haven't even started on the October monthly reports. So, seeing as you're here and I'm here, we may as well eat and go over some of this other stuff while we're at it."

Now I knew why he was bitching about Head Office. Monthly reports are *de rigueur* in the shopping centre industry, especially in a company like ours which owns and operates fourteen centres of various shapes and sizes, from small strip plazas to mega-malls, located all across the country. Managers must submit reports on sales figures, percentage rent figures, overdue rents, expenses, common area costs and the one everybody hates—vacancy rates. This figure represents a loss factor, dirty words in any business. The loss factor is the rent which would have been generated for each square foot of empty space had it been leased; in a shopping centre the size of Rosewood, it can amount to a tidy sum. The loss factor reports were used to whip the leasing people into shape at their weekly meetings.

Our Head Office bunch are so gung-ho about managers getting their reports in on time, it didn't surprise me that a couple of stray bullets and some dead people were not an acceptable excuse for tardiness.

"I'd love dinner, Bob, but we'll have to make it relatively fast. I've got something I have to do in an hour or so."

•

Nautilus Place on the mall's upper level is a pretty good seafood house. The hostess showed us to a booth at the back, dropped two menus the size of bedsheets on the table, and we settled in.

When the waiter came over, Bob ordered the Sole Amandine and I opted for Louisiana Shrimp with Creole Rice.

"Anything to drink?"

"I'll have a large ice water with two slices of lemon," I said.

"She's a cheap date." Bob looked at the waiter. "I'll have a martini. Dry, with a twist. And we're short on time, so see if you can move it along, will you?"

"Yes, sir." He ducked his head and looked a little closer at Bob. "You're the mall manager, aren't you?"

"Not at the moment. Why? Did you want to speak to him?"

"Oh, nothing important. I just wanted to say congratulations on getting a great Santa. I hear he's fabulous." And away he went.

"Is there something I'm missing here, Jenny?" Bob asked. "That's the third time I've heard that today."

"Well, you know how they all start perking up for Christmas the minute Halloween's over. I guess that's it. Nothing like rushing the seasons. And you must admit, it's a helluva lot better than being asked about the murders."

I dug around in my purse and put the video of last year's parade on the table.

"You might want to take that upstairs with you and play it in the boardroom. Everything's laid out in there for the meeting, and basically the parade'll be exactly the same as last year. The advertising schedule, the budget, the photo operation, security arrangements—it's all there."

"And when do I get to meet Santa?" Bob asked. "You know I like to do that before the whole thing starts. Make sure I'm comfortable with him." Bob was nothing if not a stickler for details.

"How about next Monday? I'll bring him in, and we'll take

him to lunch. That should give you enough time to give him your pep talk." I crossed my fingers under the table. "He's already had mine."

"Maybe we should have him at the board meeting this year. Let the directors get a gander at him, too."

I held my breath and waited, thinking fast.

"I mean, it's their money that's paying him, Jenny. What do you think?" He ran his fingers over the tines of his fork, put it down and picked up his knife to inspect that as well.

"I don't think…" Our hostess arrived with the drinks, and right behind her stood the waiter with the food. "…that's going to be too important to them, Bob. As I said yesterday, I'm convinced murder and containment will be the main topic. And I do have Christmas well in hand."

"You're right, Jenny, and of course you do. That's the problem with starting out in the business as a promotion director like I did. It might make you crazy from time to time, but you can never quite give it up."

He started picking the almond slivers off the top of his fish and, very carefully, put them all around the side of the plate.

"Bob, what are you doing? If you don't like almonds, why'd you order the Sole Amandine?"

"They're the best part, so I save them up till I'm finished everything else, then I get to eat them all at once." He found a few more under the fish, and they joined the others. "As I was saying, Jenny, don't get me wrong. I have every confidence in your handling of Christmas, but there are so many horror stories about Santa disasters in this business, and they all surface right about now. You ever hear the one about the arrival by parachute? That's my favourite."

"Yeah," I said. "It was making the rounds at the industry conference in Vegas last year. Thank God it didn't happen to me. What a nightmare. Mind you, I didn't think it was fair that the promotions fellow lost his job over it. Wonder what he's doing now?"

"If he's still in the industry and still doing promotions, I'll bet you his Santa just springs up like a mushroom on the appointed day," Bob said. "Bet there's not even a parade."

The event we were talking about had taken place in a small strip plaza just outside Niagara Falls. Santa was to arrive by helicopter, but rather than risk a real parachute jump, the promo guy had a life-sized blow-up Santa doll custom made, and this was to be thrown out of the 'copter, complete with parachute, while the real Santa waited at the back of the maintenance doors. On a signal from the manager, he would bound through and greet the kids.

At exactly ten o'clock on a bright but freezing Saturday morning, along came the helicopter. A local radio announcer stopped the tapes of Christmas music and played a drum roll over the loudspeakers on the roof of his mobile van. The very moment the dummy was tossed out, a burst of strong wind whipped up and "Santa", complete with parachute, was blown straight into the guy wires on the roof. The figure did a couple of three-sixties, got thoroughly entangled and just hung there, a mass of straps, silk and arms and legs at all angles, swaying in the breeze. Somebody on staff, forgetting about the live walkie-talkie, yelled "Santa", and the chappie in the red suit behind the doors sprang out shouting "Hi, kids. Ho, Ho, Ho!" as loud as he could.

Sitting in the restaurant, I started laughing.

"What?" asked Bob.

"I was just thinking about that story. Can you just see the kids and their parents looking back and forth from one Santa to the other? Imagine explaining that to a three-year-old. God, it gives me the willies just thinking about it."

"Me, too," Bob said. "But the good thing is, I'm feeling better now than I have for the past couple of days. And I've talked enough about Santa to do me for quite some time. Why don't you just carry on with it, Jenny? I'm sure everything's fine. Don't even bother bringing him in. If you're satisfied, then let it go…" he chuckled "…assuming, of course, I won't be hearing the whup, whup, whup of helicopter blades."

I looked at my watch. Seven o'clock, and my luck was still holding. "How'd your meeting with the mayor play? Bet he wasn't amused at being in the mall last Saturday. He's so into image and all. Wonder if the press got a shot of him in the interview room? That would ice a cake, wouldn't it?"

"Well, he wasn't too bad. He's no worse than any other politician, but if I were you, Jenny, I wouldn't ask him to judge any more events for a while."

I watched as Bob scooped up his almonds in one fell swoop.

"Actually, the main idea of the meeting with his worship was to smooth over the Stephen Jones situation. The mayor's niece is married to one of our cleaners, who apparently overheard the councillor's tirade in my office, and it got back to his honour. Jones obviously isn't the mayor's favourite person, either, but he needs him as a key player on council. On the other hand, he also needs the bucks that Rosewood produces for the city." He shrugged. "He just can't make up his mind which he needs most, I guess, so we danced around a bit then agreed to work at keeping things as low-key as we can."

The waiter came over and cleared off our plates. "Can I get you anything else? Dessert? Coffee?"

"Tea, please," I said. "No dessert."

"How about you, sir?"

"Coffee, black. And the bill."

As Bob got out his credit card and flipped it on the little tray alongside the bill, I wondered who I'd be written down as tonight. Head Office frowns on staff members taking each other out for meals, but there's always a way.

After I drained the last of my tea, I fished the Chevy keys out of my purse and got up to put my coat on.

"Bob, my mother always said it's rude to eat and run, but I really have to go. We'll have to cover the rest tomorrow. The Head Office bit I can figure out, but I'm anxious to know how your meeting with George Anderson went, and you never did tell us how you handled Councillor Jones after he broke down in your office."

"There's nothing to tell. He was just distraught, and I let him get it out, that's all."

"Anyway, we can touch base tomorrow," I said. "Talk about what's best to do about the impact of the shootings. I think I've got it figured out, but need to run it past you, see if you agree. Now, I really must leave. Thanks for dinner, it was delicious."

"Where are you off to in such a rush?"

"Just somebody I have to see, and it has to be tonight."

Bob took my arm gently, and we walked out of the restaurant. He leaned over and whispered in my ear, "Bet it's not Jim Masters."

Thirteen

Driving to the hospital, I mulled over Bob's last comment. I was in too good a mood to get overly twisted about it, but any thought of phoning Jim to try and patch things up was gone. He'd obviously told my boss about our Sunday date. Maybe not all the details, but certainly enough to cause the little smirk on Bob's face.

Too bad, but what the hell, there were probably fifty thousand guys out there I could have a decent relationship with. And probably even some among them who didn't think liver was something you should eat. One of them would come along eventually, and besides, "getting your man" has never been my idea of a meaningful life's work. Regardless of what the self-help books and the cosmetics industry say, I believe in helping myself all right, but I'll decide to what.

I was more intrigued by Tiny's fan club. First, there was the comment from Paula in the bagel shop, and now Bob was hearing the same stuff. Who else was talking? I knew the mall had a super grapevine, but even for us, this was fast. At least it was all positive. Seems I'd underrated the big guy.

The hospital parking lot was a zoo. I went around a number of times, looking for a spot big enough to avoid the danger of being dinged by another car door.

The same woman was manning the same computer as she had on Sunday, only this time her smock was yellow. "Can I help you?" she asked, as I passed her desk.

"No thanks, I know the way." I kept walking.

"But…"

I stopped. "But what…?"

"You're supposed to check in."

"I don't need a room, thank you. I'm not staying."

From the look on her face, the humour didn't register. But then, her workplace wasn't exactly a funhouse. I glanced at her name tag. "Beryl, don't worry about it. I'm here only for a minute. To visit my sister in Maternity. She's just had a little boy. Isn't that wonderful? The family is so happy."

"Congratulations," said Beryl, fingers on her keyboard. "What's her name?"

"Ivy Dhailling," I said and scooted along the hall as she peered at the screen.

Upstairs, the nurses' station was empty, and the door to Eulah Jones' room stood open. I drew myself up to my full height and walked across the hall like a person with a purpose. It's always better to look as if you have a purpose, and I wasn't going to be thwarted this time. In addition to taking umbrage at the older Jones ordering me off, I felt a real need to see this woman. Some strong emotion I didn't fully understand was pushing me towards it. Couldn't be mothering empathy—having no kids of my own—but I'd been very close with my own mother. Helen says my habit of constantly quoting her sayings is my way of keeping her near, and that's a good thing.

Maybe this thing pecking at me about Eulah Jones had something do with that. Some sort of reverse psychology. Maybe there was a little guilt because it was in Rosewood that her son got shot, and, if you spend enough time running a shopping centre, you develop a parental attitude towards it. Maybe I needed to defend my baby. Maybe a lot of things, none of which mattered. I was going to see her, and I was going to see her now.

The room was empty.

"Can I help you?"

A nurse stood in the doorway.

"I'm looking for a Mrs. Eulah Jones," I said.

"Are you a relative?"

"No. A visitor."

She moved her arm towards the hallway.

"Sorry, but you'll have to make it another time. Mrs. Jones can't be disturbed."

This was too much. What did I have to do to get to see this woman? "I don't intend to disturb her. Just visit for a bit." I started out of the room, and she followed me. "Is she over in the lounge?"

By this time, we were standing outside. She looked at me, head on one side, as if trying to decide something. "No. She's downstairs."

"Has her room been changed?"

"No. She's down in intensive care with her husband."

She stepped back to the door and pulled it shut. "Their son died an hour ago."

Fourteen

Back outside in the parking lot, I sat in the Chevy, leaning over the steering wheel, head resting on my hands, and bawling like a baby. That poor woman. Hospitalized herself, and then having to hear her son had just died. This was worse than awful.

The shootings on Saturday were bad enough, but because it had happened so fast, and with the police and all of officialdom around, there had been a vaguely surrealistic feel to it. The stuff of nightmares to be sure, but except maybe for Cathy, not my nightmare. With so much to do at the time, I suppose a certain detachment had set in, but this was different, this was real, and I was living in it.

There was a little tap-tap on the passenger side window. I looked up and saw Tiny bent over, looking in. I reached over and unlocked the door.

"Thought that was you, Miss Turnbull. Can't miss this car." He opened the door and leaned in. Dressed in a white shirt, navy pullover and grey slacks, and minus the paint smears, he looked like a real person. Not a bad-looking guy, really. "What's wrong? You find a body in this parking lot, too?"

That started the sobbing off again. I scrabbled around the floor for my box of Kleenex, but the tears were flowing so fast, I couldn't see.

"Jesus." He climbed in, threw his coat over the back of the

seat, and twisted around to face me. "I'm sorry. It was only a joke." He produced a snow-white hankie from somewhere and handed it over. "Here, use this."

I swiped at my face, raking in gulps of air, trying and failing to get some control. Tiny reached over, took the handkerchief and dabbed my face gently with one huge hand, patting my shoulder with the other.

"Please," he said softly, "try to stop."

The kindness in his voice made things worse. I took one look at him and collapsed against that massive chest. "I'm trying," I blubbered into his shirt, "but I can't seem to manage."

And so we sat. Tiny just propped me up against him, and I just cried. Eventually, I got hold of myself.

"Sorry about that." I tipped the rearview forward, took back the handkerchief and wiped my face. "I'm not normally a crybaby. Don't know what came over me."

"Sure you do," he said. "Now tell me what it was." He looked down and chuckled. "After all, it's my sweater you've just ruined."

"What are you doing here, anyway?" I couldn't risk answering him right away. The waterworks were still percolating close to the top. "Visiting somebody?"

"My father. He's having surgery tomorrow to break and reset some bones. Arthritis." He shifted his great weight around and came up with a dry handkerchief. "Start talking. What's got you in this state?"

"It's the Jones' son. Our third shooting victim. He just died."

"No shit."

"I went in to visit his mother. You know, to say how all of us were thinking about her. Tried on Sunday, but he wouldn't let me…she's been in hospital since the shooting. Fell apart.

She wasn't in her room…" The tears welled up again. "…and the nurse came and she said…" I put my head back down on the steering wheel and muttered into my hands: "It's not fair, Tiny. It's just not fair."

"What is?" he said quietly. "And who gets to decide?"

I sat up and took a couple of deep breaths. "Anyway, the whole thing just hit me when the nurse told me he'd died. I guess I was crying for all of us. For the ones who died, for the families who don't have them any more, for me 'cause I can't see my mother. It's just so horrible."

Tiny sat, not speaking, hands folded across his stomach.

"People aren't meant to go like that. Having lunch, minding your own business and zap, you're gone. Everything's over. Just like that. And now you can't say all the things you should have said. How can that happen, Tiny? How?"

The universal question. He didn't even attempt a reply. We both knew there wasn't one. We sat for a few more minutes, not talking, then Tiny opened his door. "I've got to get going, or I'll miss the bus. You be okay now?"

"You didn't drive here?"

"No, they brought Dad by ambulance because of his wheelchair and stuff, so I rode with him."

"Well, close the door. I'll drive you home. Just give me directions."

A funny look came over his face. "You okay to drive?"

"I'll be fine…" I started to say, and then I understood. "…unless you'd like to drive?" He was out of the car and round to my side before I finished the sentence. "It'll give me a chance to compose myself a bit." I slid over and Tiny got behind the wheel, turned the key and eased the car out of the parking stall.

"Tiny, thanks a lot…" he flicked his hand "and please call

me Jenny." I looked at his collar, which was now a mess of watery mascara and broad smears of lipstick. "I think, now I've wet your chest down, Miss Turnbull's a tad formal."

"No shit."

Just before the exit, I undid my seat belt and reached down to pick up a quarter from the floor. "This is the first time I've been a passenger in this car, Tiny, and I'm even getting paid for it. How about…?"

"God Almighty!" Tiny's hand clamped on my shoulder and jerked me upright. He stomped on the brakes and the car skewed to the right, coming to a stop about two feet away from Councillor Jones.

"Did you see that?" Tiny roared. "That stupid son-of-a-bitch just stepped off the curb. Wasn't even looking!" He blasted the horn. "Look at him, Jenny. He's still not even lookin'!" He put the car in park, opened the door and threw out a leg.

"Let it go." I caught his elbow. Jones kept walking, oblivious to what had just happened. "He's distraught, in shock."

"I'll give him shock and distraught. Fuckin' idiot! Let go of me." His face was turning purple. He pulled his arm free and swung the other leg outside.

"Calm down, Tiny. Please." I lunged at the back of his sweater and hung on with both hands. "The man's just lost his only son. No wonder he didn't see us. I doubt he's seeing anything right about now. Let him keep going, and we'll just sit here for a minute. Okay?"

Tony sat back, breathing hard. "You mean that jerk is Councillor Jones? The one with the dead kid? Sure looks different than the last time I saw him. No wonder I didn't recognize him."

"You know him?"

"No way, not me. I've seen him, though, and he was a jerk then, too." He wasn't quite ready to give it up.

"Tiny, what on earth are you talking about?"

"I play in a band, Jenny, once or twice a month. Jazz sax. Just for kicks and to get out for a while. A few friends—we get together and play some gigs around the area, mostly in town and mostly in small bars. I can do it after Dad's asleep, see."

This man was getting to be a bigger and bigger surprise. Jazz sax, no less.

"Go on," I said. "What about seeing Jones?"

"Well, about three or four weeks ago, Dwayne—one of the guys—booked us in to play at the Matinee Club…"

"Where's that?"

"In some little town about eighty miles north, never did get the name. Bit further than we usually go but hey, exposure is exposure. So we load the van and get there just before midnight, go in through the back and set up on stage. Place was jumping." He snorted. "Just not the way we expected."

"What way was it?"

"It was a gay bar, Jenny. Not a woman in sight. Men at the bar, men at the tables, men in leathers and feathers—you get the picture." He started the car and pulled slowly back from the curb, straightened up and headed for the exit for the second time. "But, what the hell, it didn't matter to us. We're just there to play, right?"

"Right," I nodded. "Get on with it, Tiny."

"I use the front mike in our third number, and halfway through the piece, a guy's waving at me from a table in front of the stage—it's Menard."

"Our Menard?"

"Yup. Guess he knew me from the mall. Could have knocked me down with one of their feathers. Anyway, halfway through our next piece, the front doors open, and in walks your friend. He cruises past each of the guys standing at the bar, then elbows his way across the dance floor, heading for the tables. Checks everybody out while he's at it." He stopped for a red light and looked at the dash. "We should get some gas, Jenny."

"Later. Finish your story."

"Not much to finish. Asshole there," he waved a hand back in the direction of the hospital, "drops himself in an empty seat between two other guys and waves for a waiter. Quite at home, like."

"Tiny, this is bizarre."

"No shit," he said, "especially now you've told me who he is. Anyway, we finish our first set and stop for a break. Three of us head for the bar, it's Raoul's turn to stay with our stuff. Just as we pass Jones' table, I see Menard standing beside him saying 'well, well, well'."

"And…?" I urged.

"On our way back, there's a lot of shoutin'—couldn't make it out—but the two other guys from Menard's table are beside him now, and just as we get close, your man decks one of them. One punch, and the guy's on the floor. Another punch, and Menard joins him. I tell you, Jenny, dead kid or not, that man's a nasty piece of work. Big sucker, too. Must've really hurt." The car slowed down beside an all-night gas station. "I'm pulling in here. It's not good to run a car this low. Sucks dirt into the tank. Want a chocolate bar or somethin' while I'm inside?"

"What I want, Tiny, is for you to finish the story. Now!"

"There's nothing much left." He turned off the engine and opened his door. "After a lot of shoving and pushing, two bouncers and the bartender finally got a lock on Jones and threw him out. We finished our gig and left. That's it."

After filling up, we drove in complete silence for a couple

of miles over towards Rosewood mall. I couldn't do anything but think about what I'd just heard. It was too strange for words. I had to get to Helen with this to see what she thought of it all.

"You live near the centre, Tiny?"

"Not too far," he said. "Only about a five minute drive. Works out pretty good. I can scoot home at lunch time and see to Dad."

"That's right, Ed mentioned that you live at home with your father. I take it his arthritis is severe?"

"Crippling. He's in a wheelchair. His hands are the worst. This is the second time the bones have had to be broken and reset. He says there won't be a third. Hasn't been able to feed himself for months. Can't do much of anything, really."

He eased the car over to the curb in front of a low-rise apartment building and put it in park.

"Things must be pretty hard on you, too," I said. "Can't be easy, working and seeing to your father at the same time."

Tiny stared out the window. "I manage. And besides, you can't throw people out with the trash just because they develop a few flaws." He glanced down and patted his stomach, giving me a little grin. "I've even got a few myself."

"No shit," I said.

I was liking this guy more and more. Usually, I trust my gut when it comes to first impressions of people, and with Tiny, it had been less than favourable. Our introduction hadn't exactly been under optimum circumstances, but I was fast realizing my initial take on him was completely wrong. I thought of something I'd once read about the American Civil War. Some general had said about another: "I don't like the man very much, I must get to know him better." I guess he had something.

"One more thing, Miss Turnbull…Jenny," he said, "before

I go in. Thanks for the Santa job. I really appreciate it. The extra money'll sure come in handy. I'll do a good job for you, you'll see. Those little suckers are gonna just love Santa this year."

"Tiny, you're the one doing me a favour. Maybe the extra cash can go for somebody to look after your father. You're gonna be spending a lot of hours in the shopping centre, you know."

"I thought about that last night, when Ed was telling me about being Santa. He said he knows of a few good community help programs around the neighbourhood. Going to get me some names."

"I've got some on file, too, from our Charity Bazaar and Service Club Week yearly promotion. I'll look tomorrow. Anyway, buzz upstairs when you get some time tomorrow. We'll meet and go over the whole thing then. There's just one thing I need you to start on as of now, though."

"Name it."

"I need you to stop saying 'No shit'. For six weeks, anyway."

•

Helen was upstairs folding and putting away laundry when I got home. I sat on her bed and watched her go back and forth between drawers and cupboards. She's patient and meticulous when it comes to mundane jobs—much more so than me.

"By the way, did you know Councillor Jones is gay?" I asked. She stopped in mid-stride.

"If that's some kind of joke, Jenny, I'm not laughing."

I gave her the story Tiny had told me, word for word. "What do you make of it, Helen? Shouldn't we report this to George?"

"First thing in the morning. Sure puts a new twist on things, doesn't it?"

"In my wildest dreams, I wouldn't have put Menard and

Jones Sr. in the same room, let alone in the same bar." I shook my head, trying to clear it. "This whole situation is the pits." I started matching socks from the pile in front of me and chucking the odd ones on the rug. "In fact, it'd have to jump a long way up just to get into the pits. First Cathy and Menard, then the Jones boy, and now the father could be right in the thick of it."

"I know," she said. "but as far as the son's concerned, everybody's saying it's for the best. From all accounts, he never would've recovered enough to have much of a life. Too much damage to the brain."

"That's pretty cold comfort for his mother, though," I said. "Rotten as he was, he was still her baby. She must be devastated."

She put away the last pile of underwear and sat on the edge of the bed. I got up and handed her the pile of socks. "I'm going downstairs to make us a snack."

"Didn't you eat dinner?" she asked.

"I did, but what's that got to do with a snack?"

She shook her head. "I'll be down shortly. I want to iron a blouse for tomorrow. This running back and forth between work and the cop shop is throwing my routine totally off."

"I know what you mean. If I don't do some laundry tonight, I'll have to buy new underwear tomorrow."

Our refrigerator didn't have much of anything that I could see. Even the freezer compartment looked pretty forlorn. Usually, we have a couple of baggies of muffins or some such, courtesy of Helen's baking fits. But tonight—nada. "I'm phoning for a pizza," I called upstairs, "so don't be long."

Three-quarters of an hour later, we were in the kitchen tucking into a large, double-cheese, pepperoni and green pepper pizza and washing it down with the last of the wine from the night before.

"You know…" Helen helped herself to another slice "I sure hope nobody else gets shot in the mall any time soon. I can't take any more of these late-night binges, especially with my workout routine gone to hell lately."

"Maybe tomorrow night, we'll just talk and not eat. But I was feeling so bad, and you know how it comforts me to have a little snack."

"Yeah, right. And I also know that you're not the one who has to work it off the next day. Life's just not fair."

"That's what I said to Tiny," I said.

Helen looked at me, her last bite of pizza stopping on the way to her mouth. "What was he doing at the hospital, anyway?"

"His dad was admitted. Arthritis." I told her the rest of the story between mouthfuls.

"So now you not only have a Santa, you have one with a fan club." She stood up and started to clear the table. "You know, Jenny, it's amazing. You could fall in a pile of shit and come up smelling like a rose."

I grinned. "I know. Dontcha just love it?"

Fifteen

Wednesday morning broke to a light blanket of dazzling white. Not much of a snowfall, but a good indication of what was coming. The temperature had dropped considerably, too. It was definitely time to get to that wool farm, or sheep farm, or whatever it was properly called, then get the Chev into hibernation. On the way to work, I thought of asking my new friend, Tiny, to give it the once-over before I took it off the road. Ed had said he was a mechanic by trade, and he'd certainly shown a liking for the car. The fellow who normally looked after it had bolted to Florida after last Christmas. Said he'd had enough of cold winters, and by mid-January, when we were up to our armpits in snow, I'd probably be agreeing with him, again.

I settled in my office, complete with tea tray and a couple of freshly baked bagels, just as Shirley arrived. She got her coffee, came in and sat down. I pushed over the paper bag on my desk and she helped herself to the other bagel.

"I guess you've heard by now about the Jones' son," she said.

"I was there last night. Went to visit his mother. Great timing, huh?"

"I'll say." She hooked a couple of hair strands over one ear. "How was she?"

"I didn't get in. She was down in intensive care. Apparently, he'd died about an hour or so before I got there. You may as well track the funeral arrangements for him while you're doing the others."

"You going?"

"I think all the management should be at this one, don't you? Although, with the Councillor's attitude towards us, it's bound to be a 'damned if you do, damned if you don't' situation."

Shirley slugged down the last of her coffee and stood up, holding her half-eaten bagel. Her mix and match outfit, today, was in shades of blue. Her clothes are always monochromatic, with matching shoes, but somehow they suit her, or maybe I was just used to seeing her in one colour at a time. She hasn't gone quite as far as matching contact lenses yet.

"Thanks for the treat, but I'd better be getting to it. Got to arrange with the bailiff for some lock-ups tonight," she said.

"No rents?"

"There's a few stubborn hold-outs from the group that was in here the other day, so Bob decided they'll be the example. You finished with that tray?" I nodded, and she picked it up. "Anyway," she went on, "if they don't pay today, they're out tonight."

"Makes sense to me," I said. "By the way, I need to see Bob first thing. Let me know when he gets in, would you?"

"He's got an appointment first thing," she said, smiling. "Some Italian guy who wants to trap the pigeons on the roof. Says it's more humane than the poisoned corn we put down."

"Sure it is. Then he'll take them home and eat them."

We both laughed.

"When he's free, I'll tell him you need to see him. Might be this afternoon, though."

"This aft's no good for me. My crew are starting to put the Christmas decorations up today, so I'll be kind of tied up.

Anyway, don't worry about it. I'll meet up with him sometime this morning. Right now I'm going to do a walkabout."

I spent the next hour going around both levels, dropping in on some of the merchants, chatting for a bit and sitting here and there. Everything looked pretty normal, much as it had for the last couple of days. I really couldn't detect any appreciable difference since the shooting, which made me think the police theory about "not a random shooting" was having some effect. Helen had told her staff to quote the line at every opportunity to the tenants and hope it passed along to the customers. And if Bob had had any luck at all with Jim, maybe this week's paper wouldn't trash us totally. After all, a newspaper's a business like any other. Surely the publisher had to consider his biggest revenue producer. Freedom of the press is one thing, but dollars count. Trouble is, Jim's an editorial type from way back, and they like to believe that the story content is what sells papers, not the ads. Maybe they're right but, without the advertising dollars, they wouldn't have a forum.

Thinking about the paper reminded me that I hadn't returned Jim's phone call, but I figured it wouldn't do him any harm to wait a while longer before he apologized.

•

Around eleven, on my way back upstairs, I spotted a familiar figure over by the record store.

"Good morning, Tiny. What're you up to?"

"Oh, hi." He straightened up and turned around. "Just scrapin' some gum off the floor here."

"How's your Dad? Hear anything yet?"

"He's okay. Home in a couple of days."

"Good for him. Getting your bones broken deliberately

must be a bitch. By the way, what time do you get your lunch break? Maybe I could buy you a burger, and we can do the Santa thing. That way, it won't take you off the job or interfere with visiting your Dad. Unless you're going to the hospital at lunch time."

"Nothing I can do. One o'clock's fine."

Did this guy shorten every sentence by the first one or two words? At least he hadn't said "no shit" so far.

"Okay, I'll meet you in the Food Court beside the Burger Bar. By the way, I found some names of people who might be just right for looking after your father. I'll bring the list with me."

•

My students, Roger and Vijay, were in my office when I got back upstairs.

"Hi, guys. How come you're here so early?"

"We had a couple of spares," Roger said, "so we figured on getting started at hauling out the Christmas stuff. Josh and Joe'll be here around four."

"Cool."

They looked at each other and then at the floor.

"What's that about?" I asked.

"Jenny," Vijay said, "nobody says 'cool' any more."

"Oh?"

"Yeah. The word is 'Sweet'."

I tossed him the keys to the large promo room. "Well, you two 'Sweet' your way along to storage and start unpacking the lanterns for the outside posts. They're first to go up. The cartons are all marked. And remember, be very, very careful. Don't break anything. Those lanterns cost over ten thousand dollars."

They stood up.

"Where do you want us to take them, Jenny?"

"Nowhere. Just unpack them and dust them off. The crew coming in this afternoon'll be bringing dolly's and a little forklift for the heavy stuff. Ed's guys will supply any ladders we need. Just line them up inside the door of the promo room then report to the crew foreman when he gets here."

I handed Roger a twenty dollar bill. "Have some lunch if you're finished before he's ready for you."

In addition to the usual garlands and glitter, Rosewood has an incredible Santa Land, complete with Santa's Castle, which transforms the shopping centre into a magical fairytale place for kids and adults both. It has elves in a workshop and reindeer grazing beside a huge red and gold sleigh packed with sacks of toys. Even Mrs. Claus is at home, baking cookies in a wood stove oven.

I never get tired of watching people standing and taking it all in—all three hundred thousand dollars of it, not to mention the annual cost of hiring professionals to put it all together. Then, the weekend after Christmas, they have to come back and take it all down to clean, restore and do some paint touch-ups before it goes away for another year. But it is wonderful to be part of the whole thing, and after spring, Christmas is second on my list of favourite times.

I sat for a minute, picturing the Jones household this year and remembering my first Christmas alone. Not good stuff. Death has a way of making you feel singularly mortal. That's enough, I thought, don't get maudlin. Hearing Bob's voice in the hallway, and figuring he was bidding the pigeon man adieu, I stuck my head out the door and wiggled some fingers at Shirley. She nodded, so I went along to his office and sat down to wait.

"God save me from any more bird fanciers." In he came,

impeccable as usual. His wife had the same good fashion sense, and when you saw the two of them together, you thought more of an image than a couple. "Imagine wasting nearly an hour talking about pigeons. God rot their socks."

He went around the desk, straightened a few things and sat down. "What's up?"

"Just a couple of things, Bob. I wanted to thank you again for dinner last night. It was delish…" I put a pad of paper on his desk "…and I wanted to go over, very briefly, what I think we should do about extra advertising in face of the shootings."

Bob looked at the pad, then at me and then back at the pad. "I don't see any writing on there."

"That's because there isn't any."

"Please." He leaned back in the chair, eyes closed. "Don't let's go through this headache routine again. Not twice in two days."

"Bob, I've gone over and over this since last Saturday night. Drawn up all sorts of schedules for extra print, extra signs, extra radio. All the usual stuff. But for the life of me, I can't see any benefit to it."

"So, what are you saying?"

"I've decided to do nothing. Absolutely nothing. Except, of course, what's already booked."

That got his eyes open in a big hurry. But you gotta hand it to Bob, he's a pretty cool customer. He simply placed both arms in the centre of his desk and looked at me. "And how did you arrive at that decision?"

"One, we've already blanketed just about every form of media in town. Two, I've done some extra walkabouts this week, on top of my usual schedule, and nothing seems to have changed. People are still shopping and, although the mall's quiet, it always is, just after Halloween. You know, before the Christmas kickoff.

"I've spoken to most of the tenants—at least the sane ones—and to Helen and Ed's staff. They all agree that, from what they've overheard, people are buying the police line about the shootings not being random. And just last night, Helen was saying that the police have some leads that may be promising.

"But, three—and most important—I think that pumping up our ad campaign to countermand the shootings could possibly have a negative effect. I mean, what are we going to say, 'Don't worry…chances are you won't be shot?', or even worse…" I was up and pacing now, "…do we make a big fuss about how safe Rosewood City Centre is?"

Bob just sat. At least he was listening, although I had the feeling he was somewhat distracted.

"My concern is, Bob, that if people catch on and start thinking that if we have to tell them, in a big way, that there's nothing to worry about, they might believe there really is, and we're hiding it. If that happened, it would be worse than doing nothing."

"Fine," he said.

I stopped in my tracks and looked at him. Those baby blues just looked right back.

"Fine," he said again, "but you might have a harder sell to the Board tomorrow."

"I'll handle the Board. Between Matthew Leung's notes and your support, it'll be a snap."

"I won't be there."

"What?"

"You heard. I won't be there. You're the Promotion Director, so direct. Tell them I concur with your decision and, if they have any qualms, they can call me next week."

"What if they start in about the murders?"

"Give them the police line. Refer them to Anderson. Tell them the investigation is coming along nicely. You can handle it. Maybe have Helen, or Anderson himself if he'll do it, come in and speak to them."

"Can I ask why you won't be there?"

"No."

He pushed back from the desk, got his briefcase off the floor and started filling it with file folders. Our meeting was obviously over.

"Okay," I said. "See you later."

"Actually, you won't." He closed the briefcase and headed for the door. "I'm away for a few days. I'll see you on Monday."

"But…"

"But nothing. I told you, I'm gone till Monday. I have an Assistant Manager, a Security Chief, a Maintenance Superintendent and a Promotion Director, not to mention a secretary who knows more about this building than the rest of us put together. That's enough of a line-up to keep the building running for four days without me, don't you think?"

Without another word, he was gone. I looked at my watch. Time to meet Tiny. Pumping Shirley about this would have to wait.

My lunch date was halfway through his second burger by the time I got to the Food Court. Two orders of curly fries and a large pop with two straws sat next to his elbow.

"Tiny, I was going to treat, remember?"

"S'okay, Jenny." He took another bite of burger and stuffed a few fries in with it. "Told Herb you'd be down to pay shortly. Had to start." A giant slurp of pop followed the other stuff. "Starving."

Watching him eat, my own appetite faded. Please don't let him belch, I thought. "Can I get you anything else while I'm up there?" I asked.

"Sure," he said. "One of those apple pie thingys."

We spent the next half hour mostly with me talking as Tiny inhaled his lunch. I gave him the standard run down of do's and don'ts for old St. Nick, as well as a new one I'd learned last year. "No white gloves. It scares the little kids when Santa reaches for them with white gloves on. They think the hands aren't real."

"No shit," he said. I glared at him. "Oops. Sorry. Slipped out."

"Just make sure it doesn't slip out while you're in that castle, or I'll dethrone you." We both knew that was an empty threat, but I had to keep up my end. "So what d'you say?" I asked. "Think you can handle it okay?"

"Looking forward to it. Kids are gonna love me."

I sipped my tea and stared at him. He really did have a kind face when it wasn't scrunched up and staring through my car window, and it was certainly the right shape for Santa, as was the rest of him.

"You know, I think they will," I said.

We arranged for him to pick up the Santa suits, wigs and beard after work, so he could try them all on at home.

"They're in storage at the cleaners over by the shoe repair. Just tell them I sent you in to pick them up. And one other thing, when you're on centre stage in full costume, you should wear a white T-shirt and some lightweight longjohns underneath, just in case you get a tear. Can't have hairy legs or arms showing. Buy some, and I'll reimburse you."

"Shouldn't I try it on here, so's you can see what I look like?"

"We'll do that next week. I just need to know, by tomorrow, if the suits fit. If we need to do some alterations, or even have new ones made, there isn't a lot of time left."

"Boy, there sure is a lot to this Christmas thing, isn't there?"

"More than you know, Tiny. More than you know."

He pushed back from the table and, with some difficulty, stood up and began clearing off the mess. "You finished with that cup, Jenny?"

"No." I said. "I'm gonna sit awhile and finish it. I'll talk to you later."

"Okay, but don't forget to put your cup in the garbage."

I watched him sort and dump the paper plates and pop cups in the trash container. He was very careful to put the recyclables where they belonged and finished by wiping the tray off with a paper napkin. He came back over, picked up the list of community caregiver groups and took off with a rolling gait. He'll do nicely, I thought, if only I can get him to watch his mouth. It might be only two words, but I could just see the face of some kid's mother if her little darling told Santa she was getting a bike for Christmas, and he said "No shit."

Every year, it seems, there is some problem or other with Santa, and I didn't want Tiny's favourite phrase to be the one for this year.

A hand tapped me on the shoulder. It was Jason, Herb's son from the Burger Bar. He pointed to his father, who was waving at me. "Dad wants you," the kid muttered.

I ditched my cup in the garbage—shades of Tiny's ghost—and went over.

"The office wants you." He handed me the phone.

"Jenny," Shirley said, "there are three men on their way down to look for you. You won't miss them. They look like something from a biker club. Apparently, they're here to put up the decorations."

Just as she finished, three guys matching her description came around the corner of the Food Court. I hung up and waved them over.

Since last year's crew had had a bit of difficulty with the

larger pieces of Christmas decorations, I'd told Charlie, the crew chief, to make sure at least a couple of his people this year were a little more suited to heavy work.

And here they were, all in their twenties, I'd guess, complete with tattoos, assorted pony-tails of differing lengths and black T-shirts, sleeves rolled up over considerable-sized muscles. I noticed though, other than the universal uniform, they were clean and tidy, so that was a plus.

"You Turnbull?" one of them asked.

One of his compadres turned and punched him on the arm. "Look around, asshole. You see anybody else with hair that red?"

"I'm Jenny Turnbull, yes. And just what can I do for you fellows?"

"We're here to do them lantern things."

"Where's Charlie?"

"He got held up at our last job, but he'll be here soon as he's done. Wants we should start."

"Have you guys put up decorations before?" I could just picture one of them up a ladder and the other two throwing the lanterns up to him. Ten thousand dollar signs flashed before my eyes.

"No problem. Just tell us where you want them."

Well, beggars can't be choosers, and the decorations did have to go up. "Let's go."

With the three of them flanking me, I felt like the masthead on an ocean-going liner as we cut a swathe through the mall in four-four timing. I noticed that anybody coming towards us quickly two-stepped to one side. It was easy to see how guys like these develop that swagger they all have and, truth be told, I couldn't help swaggering a bit myself.

"Ed, you got a minute?" I poked my head in his office.

"Sure." He looked up from a pile of blueprints spread out

over his desk. "C'mon in."

Telling the monoliths to stay put, I went in, closed the door behind me and told Ed the situation.

"So you see," I finished up, "I'm a little concerned about just giving them free rein. Could you, sort of, oversee them for me? Just till Charlie arrives?"

"No can do, Jenny." He pointed at his desk. "I've got major problems with the roof units over the supermarket's bakery area. It could become an emergency with very little coaxing, so I can't spare the time."

He rerolled the blueprints and stuck them under his arm. "Besides," he went on, "surely they can't be that bad. You'll handle it."

"Take a look."

He opened the door a fraction, peeked out and closed it very quietly. "Tell you what. Since he's already sucked into this Christmas business, I'll lend you Tiny for the rest of the day. That's the best I can do."

"Tiny's better than nothing, I guess. I just hope he's okay with these guys. He's kind of a softie at heart, you know. And they look pretty formidable. I don't want some kind of pissing contest to start." I shrugged. "I have no other answer. Where is he?"

Ed tossed a walkie-talkie across the desk and left. I paged Tiny, who said he'd be there right away. Must've been doing something he was anxious to leave. More gum, maybe.

"Meet you in the yard."

"No, Tiny, come straight into Ed's office. I want a word with you, in private, about what you'll be doing."

A few minutes later, bedlam broke out on the other side of the door. I punched the transmit button on the radio.

"Helen…come to Ed's office. Quick. Helen…Ed's office. Security…anybody."

The noise was getting louder. What the hell could be happening? Should I open the door? Should I wait for Helen? I finally jerked it open and there were Tiny and the giants, grinning like crazy, shouting and pounding each other on the arms, backs and anywhere else they could land a punch.

"Tiny," one of them yelled, "you old son-of-a-bitch."

"No shit," shouted one of the others.

"How they hangin', babe?" This one's voice could be heard into the middle of next week.

I went back into the office, picked up Ed's metal waste basket and thwanged it off the door a couple of times. "Shut the fuck up!"

That got their attention. The four of them stood, rooted in place, and stared at me.

"Wow," one of them said, "she's wicked!"

"That voice could boil water," another one added.

I glared at them and held onto the wastebasket. "What the hell is going on here? Are you all bloody nuts?"

A grin as wide as the Grand Canyon split Tiny's face.

"Tiny, you know these people?"

"They're my buds, Jenny. From way back." He turned and threw an arm across the nearest one's shoulders. "What're you guys doin' here?"

Before they could answer, Helen and Carson, one of her guys, came around the corner on the run, pulling up short when they saw our little group.

"What's going on here?" Helen asked. "What's the trouble, Jenny?"

After we had everybody quietened down and sorted out, it turned out that Tiny and the three guys were old buddies. He used to work on their cars and bikes at his old job, and they had become fast friends, but because of his home situation and new place of employment, he hadn't seen them for quite some time.

Helen and Carson eventually left, her shaking her head at me, and as old home week seemed to be over, I got Tiny and his trio filled in on what they were to do, then went back into Ed's office to sit down and try to recover from the excitement.

"Jenny?" the radio crackled. Shirley's voice. "You hear me, Jenny?"

I pressed the button. "Go ahead."

"You're needed in the office. I've got a problem."

I looked at my watch. Barely two-thirty, and I felt like an elephant hanging over a cliff with its tail tied to a daisy. "What is it now? No, never mind. I'm on my way up."

I scribbled a little note for Ed, thanking him for giving me Tiny for the afternoon, and made my way back upstairs and into the office. Shirley was alone, so at least the problem wasn't sitting on the couch.

"What's happening, bro?" I asked her.

"Well, you know I was arranging for some lock-ups for after closing tonight?"

"Right. You were gonna do that this morning. Something go wrong?"

"Big time," she said. "The guy who owns the leather goods store…"

"Santillo. The one with the mouth," I said.

"…well, it seems, and don't ask me how, but it seems he found out about the hit list and that he was on it."

"And…?"

"And he's moved a sleeping bag in. He intends to camp out in the store till we change our mind."

"That'll never happen. Remember Bob's little speech, Shirley?"

"But we can't lock him in the store. That's unlawful confinement. We can't do it."

"True enough. But what do you want me for?"

"Well, Bob's gone until Monday, and Keith's not here, so you're in charge. I thought maybe you could go down and have a word with him."

"Fat chance. I might be in charge, but I'm not suicidal. That little sucker's got a nasty temper, and besides, if he wants to spend a night or two in his store, who are we to talk him out of it? I, personally, don't give a rat's ass if he sleeps in there for the next year. Let him get on with it. I guarantee you, his mind'll change long before Bob's does. I'm going back out into the mall to check on what's happening with the decorations. I hope Charlie's here by now. If I'm not back when the other kids arrive, just send them out to look for us. In the meantime, cancel the order to lock up Santillo."

I stopped halfway to the door. "By the way, Shirley, if you see Keith before I do, tell him I won't be in on Saturday, so he's to cover."

I stopped again. "That reminds me. One last thing. When I get back, I want to hear all about Bob's sudden departure."

"Jenny, I can't…"

I scooted out the door. "See ya."

•

By eight o'clock, the Christmas decorations were well in hand, and Charlie figured they'd be finished by the start of the coming week.

"I tell you, Jenny," he said, "I'd give anything to have that Tiny guy on my gang. He might be a bit chubby, but he's sure got staying power. Worked like a dog all afternoon."

We were on a bench going over the schedule for the next couple of days and watching Charlie's people put some finishing touches on the reindeer area. Tiny was right in there with the rest of them.

"Touch him, Charlie," I said, "and you're dead. If you even breathe on him, I'll lay you out."

He grinned. "Well, I guess we're in the right place for that kind of threat, aren't we?"

"Very funny." I stood up. "How late do you think you'll be tonight?"

"Another couple of hours should do it. We'll be back first thing tomorrow."

"Okay. I'm going home now, so I'll see you in the morning."

•

Helen came into the boardroom just as I was eyeballing the set-up for tomorrow's meeting.

"You about finished?" she asked.

"Five minutes, and I'm outta here. By the way, can you come into the meeting tomorrow for a few minutes and update the board on how the investigation's going?"

"Why me?" she said. "Shouldn't you and Bob handle that?"

"He's away till Monday." Her eyebrows went up. I held up a hand. "Don't ask, because I don't know. He wouldn't say, and try as I might, Shirley won't talk. I couldn't get a word out of her. Must be serious for her to clam up like that. Anyway, can you do it? They're definitely gonna ask about the shootings, and I'll need all the backup I can get. Particularly as I don't know much more than they do. That reminds me, what did George say when you told him about our favourite politician and his strange friends?"

Helen moved back over to the door, opened it and looked up and down the hall. Closing it again, she sat down and gestured for me to do the same.

"I'll do your meeting tomorrow. But here's what we're not gonna tell them." Her voice was low, and she kept looking at the door.

"For God's sake, Hel, what's all the cloak and dagger stuff?" I asked. "You're making me nervous."

"First, you are not to breathe a word of this, not one word. Okay?"

"Okay."

"I mean it, Jenny."

"Cross my heart and hope to die tomorrow. Now talk."

She took the walkie-talkie out of her jacket pocket and set it on the table.

"Remember I told you the other night that the cops were looking into a couple of rumours they heard on the street…about a connection between Menard and the Jones boy?"

"Yeah, and…"

"Well, they're still working that angle, and seems they've all but got the connection made, but yesterday, Hobart walked in with the news that Dan Haggerty has been playing kissy-face with the woman who manages the jewellery store downstairs."

"What?" I shrieked. "Cathy's husband?"

Helen darted over to the door and took another quick peek outside. "For God's sake, Jenny, keep your voice down."

"We're safe as houses in here." I shook my head. This was too much. "I can't believe this."

"Apparently, it's been going on for some time," she said. "Hot and heavy. I'm as surprised as you are. What I can't figure out is how the mall grapevine missed this one. In fact, I don't even know how Hobart dug it up."

I sat back in the chair and stared at her. I'm not often at a loss for words, but this was almost as much of a stunner as Tiny's story. I'd only met Haggerty a couple of times in their store, and he'd struck me as a nice but ordinary type of guy. Pleasant enough, a bit on the shy side, and certainly no oil painting.

"I guess my mother was right," I said.

"Right about what?"

"She always said the quiet ones were the worst."

"The worst what?"

"I don't know. She never said."

Helen stood up and picked up her two-way. "And now we've thrown the Councillor's story into the middle. God knows which way things are going to go now. I gotta get going, get the night crew briefed. This extra shift since the murders has really put a dent in my Security budget."

I stood up fast. "Oh, no you don't. You can't drop a bombshell like this and just leave. I want to know all of it."

"That is all of it. George's bunch are going to follow it up, and, from what I gathered earlier, they've split their team in two. One group'll continue the Menard-Jones angle, and the other is assigned to explore this new development about Haggerty. Then there's last night's addition. He'll have to put a team on that, too. I was thinking, Jenny, maybe Menard was blackmailing Jones Sr.? All this sure puts a different slant on things, doesn't it?"

"I'll say. This is exciting. D'you think Cathy's husband could be the shooter? Maybe he was trying to get rid of her because of his girlfriend." I stood up and gathered up my stuff. "Maybe Cathy found out. Maybe it was the girlfriend. Has sex reared its ugly head? Tune in tomorrow and find out."

Helen opened the door. "Stuff it, Jenny. And remember, not one word."

Sixteen

Helen was as good as her word. She not only made the Board meeting, but came in accompanied by George Anderson himself and, since she hadn't come home last night, I assumed she hadn't had too far to go tracking him down. Both of them looked a little haggard. Must have been a late night.

When everyone was settled, I brought the meeting to order and gave the directors Matthew Leung's regrets, a copy of his notes and a short speculative version of Bob's absence—"family matters" is always good—then covered off the Christmas promotion pretty quickly. It wasn't hard, since their eyes had locked on George the minute he had walked in and stayed there. I could have been a potted plant for all the attention my plans got. I could only hope they wouldn't recap when they got their copy of the minutes later in the day and change their minds about agreeing to everything. Maybe Shirley would be too busy for the next few days to type them up.

"That's the end of my presentation, ladies and gentlemen." I stacked my papers into a neat pile. "As you can see, Christmas is well in hand. The decorations will be up by the beginning of next week and then there's just the parade and Santa's arrival for next weekend, both of which are primed and ready."

Even to myself, I sounded good.

"Inspector Anderson will now give you an update on the investigation into last Saturday's events, and that will bring our meeting to a close."

George stood up and took about ten minutes to tell them absolutely nothing they hadn't already heard. He stressed the fact that he had two teams working on two different angles, but would not elucidate when asked by one of the department store managers. He did say that he felt strongly an arrest was imminent but, of course, was "not at liberty to provide details" as the "investigation was ongoing" and ended by saying again that, due to certain information in their hands, the police department was convinced the shootings were not a random act.

I looked at Helen, but her expression didn't change one whit.

"I have stressed this in all our meetings with the press and shall continue to do so," he went on. "In fact, I'm quoted in today's issue of *The Weekly Times* as having said just that. And now, if you'll excuse me?"

He came over, shook my hand, then turned to Helen. "Ms. Lemieux, can I see you in your office for a few minutes?"

The room emptied pretty quickly after they left. I looked at my watch. Ten-thirty, and we were done—a record. But I left wondering just what the police thought the motive really was for the murders.

Too bad things in the office weren't running as smoothly. Poor Shirley was fending off three of her "lock-ups". Just as I was opening the door, one woman was threatening to sue the mall owners for interfering with her right to conduct business or some such stupid expression. Lawsuits were quickly becoming the threat of choice around here.

"I want my store reopened, and it'd better be now." Her voice got shriller by the minute. "You have absolutely no right to do this. None."

"Actually," I said as I walked over to her, "we do. Have the right, that is. Read your lease. We also have the right to have you removed from this office if you don't stop harassing our staff."

"Harassing your staff?" Her voice went up another couple of octaves. "What do you call changing the lock on my store, and what do you call posting a notice in the window saying I've been locked up for not paying my rent? What do you call that?"

"Legal," I said. I put out my hand. "Shirley, the envelope please."

She opened a drawer and handed me an envelope with the new keys and tags for the closed-out stores. I turned back to the rebellion.

"All of you were notified by Mr. Graham that refusal to pay your rent would result in your being locked out. You were further advised that the account must be settled by certified cheque before you will be permitted to re-enter your premises…"

One of the men cut in. "I want to talk to Graham. He can't do this."

"…he can, he did and you can't. He's away until Monday and I, being only the Promotion Director, don't have the authority to change his decisions. However, if you want to come back with either cash or a certified cheque, I'll be happy to give you the new keys to your store."

The three of them left with a good deal of muttering and harrumphing, but we had them, and they knew it. They'd be back with the money before another hour was out.

"Smart move on Bob's part, Shirl, to take these particular days off."

"Wasn't it, though?" She grinned and headed for the kitchen. "Thanks for taking them off my hands. I'm going to make a pot of tea. Want a cup, Jenny?"

I followed her up the hall. "I take it the others have coughed up, but what happened with Santillo? He spend the night?"

"He did. Stupid idiot. Keith's down there talking to him now, but I bet he won't get very far." She filled the teapot while I set out the cups. "I think this is going to be a Mexican stand-off until Bob gets back."

"Works for me," I said.

"But the best story," she went on, "is that woman who was just in here bitching the loudest. According to Peter, when she arrived to open the store and saw the bailiff's notice, she covered it with a large piece of paper taped to the window that read 'Closed for Inventory'. Clever of her."

"After the fact, though. If she was really smart, she'd have paid her rent in the first place. Are they ever gonna realize they simply can't win?" I rinsed out my cup and put it away. "I'm going out in the mall for a while."

"By the way, Jenny, how'd your meeting go?"

"Piece of cake. See you in a bit."

A quick trip around the mall showed everything pretty much cooking right along. There were customers on both levels, Christmas decorations had popped up here and there, and things were looking pretty good. I got a copy of *The Weekly Times* from the newspaper kiosk, a cup of tea from the food area and sat down to read what it had to say.

The story, as expected, was on the front page, but at least there were no screaming headlines, I guess because the news was nearly a week old. Bob's damage control meeting with Jim must have been successful to a certain extent, as the story was pretty straightforward and factual, finishing up with George's quote and a line that said "cont'd on page 5". That turned out to be a picture spread with a half-dozen or so shots, in full living colour, mostly taken in the Food Court.

I could have done without the one of some little kids backed into a corner, and I didn't find the one of Joe up on the table in my sweatsuit too amusing, but the most damaging ones, for us, had to be of a distraught mother hugging her little boy, and another showing a bloody shoe lying beside a pedestal table.

There was also one of Councillor Jones and his wife, obviously taken during his last election campaign. At least, I assumed it was his wife. She was standing behind the great man, one hand through his arm with only the left side of her face showing and looking like she was ready to bolt.

That reminds me, I thought, I must call her and offer my condolences. I looked at the Councillor's picture again. And if you don't like it, tough shit.

I folded the paper and put it down just as Keith came over and sat down.

"What do you think?" He thumbed through the paper.

"All in all, not too bad," I said. "Could have been a lot worse. Think what it would've been like if the shootings were yesterday? And, at least they didn't put the pictures on the same page as our ad. Remember when they had a picture of the guy who was murdered in a poker game brawl right next to an ad for a funeral home? You want a coffee or anything?"

"No thanks," he said. "I was just doing my rounds and saw you sitting here."

"How'd you make out with Santillo?" I asked. "Shirley said you'd gone down to talk to him."

"Guy's an idiot," he said. "Said he has to stand on his principles."

"Sleep on them, you mean," I said. "Oh well, when Bob gets back he'll have him out in a nanosecond."

"What's with all of you taking off anyway? First Bob's gone, then I hear you're not coming in this weekend. What's going on?" He took off his glasses and held them up to the light, shaking his head. "These lenses are scratched to shit. So much for paying extra for non-glare coating."

"For Pete's sake, Keith, Bob's not 'gone', he's only away until Monday, and I'm simply taking Saturday off. It's no big deal."

"What's so important about Saturday?" He just couldn't let it go. "You and Jim got a hot date?"

"Something like that," I said. "I do have a life, after all, Keith. One that doesn't include this shopping centre."

"Yeah, sure," he said. "Like we all do."

He was absolutely right, of course. Once you spend a couple of years in the shopping centre business, you're done like dinner. It takes hold and never lets go until you either quit or peg it—and probably not even then.

"Excuse me…"

I looked up. A woman was standing beside our table holding on to an empty shopping cart.

"…are you Miss Turnbull? She said you were skinny with frizzy red hair."

Keith stood up, muttering something about seeing to a problem with the heating system.

"Yes, I'm Jenny Turnbull. Can I help you with something?"

"I've got a complaint—about one of your stores."

"And what would that be, Mrs…?"

"Morrison." She drew herself up to all of five foot two. "Mrs. Morrison."

"Won't you sit down? Or perhaps you'd prefer to come up to my office?"

"I'll stand just fine," she said.

I'll bet you will, I thought. "What can I help you with?"

"It's about a sweater I wanted to buy, and the store wouldn't sell it to me."

"Oh?"

"Yes. Oh."

I sighed inside. This was like pulling teeth. Why can't people learn to speak right out?

"And…?" I encouraged.

"I went into that ladies' wear boutique down beside the sports goods store, and they wouldn't sell me the sweater I wanted. I had the money out and everything."

"That's odd," I said. "Did they say why?"

"No," she said. "They just said they wouldn't sell it to me, so I went to the Information Booth to complain, and they said to see you."

"The skinny one with the red frizzy hair," I said, trying to raise a smile. "Well, Mrs. Morrison, this doesn't sound quite right. This is the first complaint we've ever had about that particular store. Leave me your phone number, and I'll check into it with the store manager and call you later today."

She folded her arms across her chest. "I'll wait."

"It might take some time. I have something else to do first."

"I'll wait."

When I left, she was still standing beside the cart. Hadn't moved an inch. I hightailed it down to the store, hoping she wouldn't change her mind and follow me. It turned out she was right. The store manager had refused to sell her the sweater. But, of course, it wasn't that simple.

The real story was that she'd seen the sweater on display in the window and went in to buy one, only to find they didn't have her size in the colour she wanted. The only one to fit the bill was the one in the window, and they weren't prepared to take it out.

"I tried explaining to her, Jenny, that we pay hundreds of dollars to have our windows professionally dressed, and that even our staff aren't allowed to touch them, but she just wouldn't listen," the store manager explained. "Said she wanted that one, and she wanted it right then. I told her the only thing I could do was guarantee she could have it next month when the display is changed. That wasn't good enough, and she got quite ugly about it, so I asked her to leave the store. Sorry, but that's the way it is."

"It's not for you to apologize," I said. "Don't worry about it. I'll go back and have a word with her and let you know later whether to keep it for her next month or not."

There was no sign of Mrs. Morrison in the Food Court, though the empty cart was still beside the table. I guess she'd changed her mind about waiting and gone home. Just as well. I'd had enough upstairs and wasn't in the mood to argue with any more stubborn people.

I walked over to the door beside the Chinese food outlet that led into the back hall, went through and yelled "get a life, people" as loud as I could. It felt good but brought the cook running to see what the noise was.

"What's wrong, Miss Jenny?" His fist was clenched around a wicked-looking cleaver. "Why you yell?"

"It's okay, Sammy." I patted his shoulder. "It's okay. Police business. They asked me to check the noise level in the hallway. That's all. Thanks for looking out for me though."

"S'okay, Miss Jenny. I like. You yell, I come quick. Catch killer."

Now there was a plan. Lure the killer into the back hall, yell loudly and let Sammy take care of the rest. It had a few flaws but, overall, I could see it working. I'd have to run it past George.

•

"Speak of the Devil and he's sure to appear" was another one of my mother's little insights, and sure enough, he was in my office when I got back upstairs.

"Hi, George," I said. "You and Helen finished your meeting? You need me for something?"

"Not really, Jen…" Jen? I thought. How sweet. What's this gonna cost? "…I'm on my way back to the station and thought I'd drop by to say hello first. We haven't had much of a chance to talk lately. Informally, that is. How've you been?"

"Never better, George, and neither is Helen. Although these murders are taking their toll on her, what with all the extra hours she's been putting in. Seems as if she's hardly ever home any more."

I had to hand it to him. His expression was locked on. Not a single muscle twitched.

"So she tells me," he said pleasantly enough. "But, as you no doubt know, we do have a couple of promising leads. I'm pretty confident we'll be making an arrest soon. Just a matter of days."

He stood up, ready to leave, and out popped the reason for our cozy little tête-à-tête.

"By the way, I'm sure Helen's told you I've asked her to think about moving back in to our apartment? Start again, you know?"

He hesitated, and I just sat there, looking up. He sure was gorgeous, and I could certainly see the attraction for Helen—that is, if looks were the only thing. But ego was quite another, and his didn't show too many dents. Come to think of it, neither did Jim's.

"I was wondering what you thought about that, Jenny. What you've said to Helen? I know you two are like sisters."

"Closer." I stood up, took his arm, and we walked up the hall together. "To tell you the truth, George," I said, "Helen and I don't discuss you at all, unless, of course, we're talking about the murders, so I'm afraid I really can't help your cause." I held the door open for him. "But do drop by any time, here or the house. It's always good to see you."

•

After he left, I made an executive decision to just hang for a half-hour or so, get some peace and quiet. I told Shirley to nix the phone then shut the door, took off my shoes and sat back in one of the visitor chairs with my feet stuck up on the desk. Over in the corner, my poor little knitting bag sat looking pretty forlorn. Mrs. Morrison wasn't the only one who couldn't get the sweater she wanted, but at least I wouldn't have to wait quite so long for mine. Roll on, Saturday. I get really antsy when I don't have knitting of some kind on the go. I always seem to be able to think things through better when I'm watching the needles clacking along.

I've often wondered why more people don't take it up, especially men. Years ago in the middle east, young boys stood on hillocks, knitting away while they watched their herds of goat or sheep and, if you've ever watched a sailor mending nets, it's not a big leap to see how string bags came into being. I thought, not for the first time, how much we'd all lost by defining man's work and woman's work over the centuries.

Thinking about work, and a knock on the door, brought

me out of my reverie. Time to get back to it.

"Come in." I scrambled to get my shoes back on and went around the desk to my usual chair.

"Relax, Jenny, it's just me." Shirley—green outfit today—came in with a message slip. "This call's from the Strawberry Farmers Guild in Mayville, that little town north of here. They want to know if you'll be one of the judges for next summer's Strawberry Queen contest."

"Shirley." I started laughing. "It's November, for God's sake."

"I know," she said, "but they need to know now, something about starting early."

"I'll say. Do me a favour, call them back and say I'd love to be a judge, and they should send the info when it's ready. Date, times, etc."

She went back to her desk and I sat there, still chuckling, and thinking "and the beat goes on."

•

Out in the mall, Charlie and his gang, along with my boys, were hard at work stringing garlands and lights around the Centre Court area. There was no sign of Tiny. I guessed Ed had decided his sabbatical was over and snapped him back to Maintenance.

We'd decided to put Santa's castle up last, so that wouldn't happen until next Wednesday or Thursday. It's hard to keep kids—and a fair number of adults—from poking around in there once it's in place. The year before, we'd had to repaint it a couple of days before the parade and then pray it dried in time. I wasn't about to go through that again. Our game plan this year was to put all the higher-up decorations in place first where they couldn't be fidgeted with, or plucked at, or even downright stolen, all of which happen quite often. The Easter before, we'd had three large plaster toadstools stolen from our Easter Bunny display. It hadn't bothered me too much. I'd never liked them from the day they arrived. Whoever had made them had a warped sense of humour. They were the most phallic-looking mushrooms I've ever seen, and not exactly appropriate for a kids' event, but they'd only arrived the day before our promotion, and there wasn't enough time to send them back for a retrofit. The next year, I went with leprechauns.

"Looking good, Charlie," I said.

"Thanks, Jenny." He climbed down from his ladder. "I sure miss that Tiny guy, though."

"Can it, Charlie. I told you. He's not available, and he's not going to be. Not if you want to keep the Rosewood contract, that is."

"Miss Turnbull, are you threatening me?"

"Damn straight I am. Want a bagel and juice?"

He wiped both hands on his coveralls and took off his tool belt. "Bribery now. I wonder what it'll be next."

"It won't be anything next. Let's go." I pointed at the roll of drawings lying on his workbench. "And bring those with you so we can go over them again. I want to make sure you're keeping on top of my schedule."

Charlie scrunched up his face and tried his best to leer. "I'll keep on top of anything of yours, Jenny."

"Stuff it, Charlie. You tried all your moves on me last year, and they didn't work then either. You're a nice guy but, trust me, it ain't gonna happen."

"Okay, then," he said, "I'll settle for the bagel."

•

There was a note on my desk from Helen asking if I wanted to meet her for dinner "somewhere off-site, I've had enough of this place for today." According to her scribble, she'd be in court this afternoon, but I should leave a message at the Info Booth "if I decided to join her."

Strange she left a note, I thought. She's never had a problem finding me before when she needs to. And what's this shit about "deciding to join her?" Why so formal? This is me she's talking to.

I didn't like this. Not one bit. I read the note again. It felt wrong. This had to do with George.

Seventeen

We never did meet for dinner, at least not in a restaurant. I left a message for Helen saying I'd see her around eight at a little family-owned Italian ristorante not too far from the house. Still concerned about the tone of her note, I drove home to squeeze in a quick shower and change before heading over to the eatery.

I opened the back door and stepped into the Twilight Zone.

The kitchen table was covered with cans, boxes, bottles, bags of flour, bags of sugar, plates, cups and saucers, glassware and everything else that had been in the cupboards, whose doors all stood open. The floor was dotted with piles of pots and pans and all the cleaning stuff, and junk from under the sink was strewn across the counter top. The only thing that didn't seem to have been opened and emptied, at least as far as I could tell, was the fridge. All told, it was not a pretty sight.

In the middle of all this chaos stood two fat, blonde pups, no bigger than a thimble, busy pulling a piece of bread apart. They looked up as I came in, and two chubby rear ends started wagging like crazy, but they didn't let go of the bread.

"Hi, guys," I said. "Helen around?"

"I'm here," She came down the back stairs, crossed the room to the rocker, sat down and burst into tears. One of the pups let go of the bread and joined in, howling fit to beat the band, and the other one, not to be outdone, put in its two cents worth too.

Taking a couple of steps backward and leaning on the still-open door, I started howling myself, but they were howls of laughter. Probably not the right move, but I just couldn't help it. This was just too bizarre, even for this household. The dogs immediately stopped their caterwauling and charged in my direction. I picked them up, tucked one under each arm and sat down opposite Helen.

"Dinner ready?" I asked. "I can see you've been slaving over a hot stove, so I assume you changed your mind about a restaurant?"

She rolled down the sleeve of her shirt, wiped her face on it and glared at me. "It's not fucking funny, so shut up!" she shouted. "Why do you have to make a joke out of everything? I'm tired of it, d'you hear me, Jenny? Tired of it. And put those fuckin' dogs down before they pee on your skirt."

"Too late," I said. "They already have, both of them it feels like."

She swiped at her face a bit more and leaned over to poke around the ashes from last night's fire. "Oh, Jenny, I'm sorry. I shouldn't have yelled at you. This isn't even about you."

"Well, that's a relief," I said. "You had me worried there for a minute. What is it about, exactly?"

"I guess it's about George and what he wants. And it's about me and not knowing what I want. Not for sure, anyway."

"That's usually not a problem for you."

She hunched back over her lap and starting crying again. Quietly this time, which was even worse. I leaned over and patted her knee, almost squishing the pups.

"And I'm sorry for laughing. It wasn't at you, it was just at the whole thing." I turned to take another look at the room. "You have to admit this is a bit beyond pasta primavera and bruschetta at the Taste of Italy."

"Things just caved in on me on the way home, I guess." The tears were still running down her cheeks. She took a huge breath and sat up straight. "You're right, it isn't like me. Sometimes I just get tired of being the strong one. All my life I've had to be strong for one reason or another. 'Look after your brothers', 'look after your father', 'look out for the aunts, cousins, uncles, whoever'—seems that's all I ever heard, growing up."

She got up and started to mindlessly put stuff back in cupboards. The dogs and I just stayed where we were and let her get on with it.

"George is really pushing me to move back in with him. Between that and the pressure of these murders and still having to cope with the normal security problems at work—we actually arrested some woman trying to steal a sweater out of a window display this afternoon. Can you believe it?"

She looked around the kitchen. "Guess I thought a bit of no-brainer housework would help me forget about all the stuff that's making me crazy." She lifted her hands. "I started on one cupboard, and it kinda just went from there. D'you know we've got four half-empty bags of sugar?"

"Doesn't surprise me," I said. "Go on about our Georgie. Are you leaning in any particular direction?" I crossed my fingers under the pups where she couldn't see them.

"Well, that's just it. I don't know. What do you think I should do?"

"Oh, no. Don't look at me. You'll have to go it alone on this one. But I do have one question."

"What?" She stopped and turned to face me. She looked really pitiful.

"Do you really want to go back to what you left? Don't

answer that now. Think on it for a while."

I put the pups down and got to my feet, rolling up my sleeves. "In the meantime, let's get at least some semblance of normalcy back in here. You do the top cupboards, I'll handle the bottom." I looked down at the dark patch on my skirt. "Then I have to take a shower."

She came over and put her arms around me, squeezing tight. I held on to her just as tightly and patted her on the back.

"Don't say it, Helen," I said. "Just clean. But when you're ready to talk, I do have just one more question."

She dropped her arms and stood back to look at me.

"Exactly what are we doing with two dogs?" The pups were lying like rugs under the table, sound asleep. It was hard to tell where one stopped and the other one started. "Don't get me wrong. They're really cute, but what are they doing here? Whose are they?"

"They're ours, Jenny. You know we've always talked about getting a pet. Well, now we've got two. Peter found them in a cardboard box in one of the back hallways. Somebody dumped them." The first smile I'd seen in a couple of days flashed across her face. "Aren't they cute? One can be yours, and the other one can be mine, or they can both be ours. You can even knit little coats for them. Use up your scrap wool. What d'you think?"

"I think you've made up your mind, that's what I think. And stop rattling. You're beginning to sound like me."

She stood at the sink, looking out the window, although it was so dark outside she couldn't possibly see anything.

"This isn't about little coats, Helen, or scraps of wool or even little pups. I remember you told me on more than one occasion that George doesn't like animals, and that he lives in a 'no pets and no kids' apartment by choice, and you come home with not just one, but two dogs?"

Silence reigned while we stacked and tidied and wiped. She was deep in thought, and I'd said enough. At least she'd stopped crying, thank God. I can't stand it when Helen's upset. After a long few minutes of silence, she came out of it. "Look, we're nearly done now. I'll finish up while you go have a shower, and then I'll make us an omelet. After we eat, we can talk about what to call the pups."

"Besides ours, you mean?"

She snapped me on the backside with the end of a tea towel, and I headed up the hall.

•

After supper, we sat back and looked at the newest additions, still out like a light under the table.

"I'd have thought the smell of food would've brought them to their feet," I said. "You know, Helen, that's a lot of responsibility you've just brought home. Are you sure we're ready to be parents?"

"Absolutely," she said. "We always had dogs around when I was a kid, and you've told me often enough about your granny's old sheepdog—the one she buried in the backyard and you and your sister made a little cross for. This old house will seem more like a home with them in it. Just think about the welcome we'll get after a bad day."

"Okay. Names, then. What d'you fancy?"

"I think we should just have one name between the two of 'em. When we call one, we're gonna get both anyway. I don't think we have to decide tonight, though. Let's leave it till they've been here a while. Something's sure to strike us eventually."

She got up and lifted them from under the table, handling

them like an old pro. They didn't wake up until she was at the door and the cold air hit them.

"I'm gonna put them outside for a whiz. You want to go to a movie when I'm done? Take our mind off things?"

"I've got a better idea. I think we should go to the funeral home for Gerry Menard and Cathy Haggerty."

"What?" she almost shrieked. "Is that your idea of a distraction?"

"Think about it, Helen. We have to make an appearance sometime, and Cathy's funeral's tomorrow. I was planning on going, but since you told me about her sleazeball husband, I can't face looking at him for that long. I'd rather just go to the viewing tonight, pay my respects and then leave. Even so, it'll be hard to look at him and not say anything, but if we go at night, there's sure to be a number of people there, so maybe we won't even have to say anything. Just nod, sign the book and run.

"And as for Menard, it's the same funeral home—isn't that handy—and, according to Shirley, the service is family only. All we have to do is pop into their viewing room and sign their visitors' book, too. That way we can kill two birds with one stone." I clamped a hand over my mouth. "My God, I can't believe I said that."

Helen held the door open and the blonde bullets hurtled in, dashed across the floor and back under the table. They flopped back down and started a game of "chew my ear and I'll bite your paw." The thought struck me that my knitting bag had better find a new home. The floor was not going to be safe any more.

"Other than that piece of bread they were mauling when I came in, have those two eaten?"

"Yep," Helen said. "I bought some puppy chow on the way home. They're fine for tonight."

"And have you organized their sleeping quarters too?"

"Not yet." She actually grinned. Quite a change from an hour ago. "I thought you could take on that little task."

"Get your coat, and let's get the hard job done first."

"You start the car, and I'll put the pups in the bathroom."

•

I parked in the funeral parlour front lot and felt Helen tense up the minute I turned off the engine. She detests funeral homes and everything about them and has been pretty successful at avoiding them for most of her life up to now. Says it's the Indian in her. Once, when she was asking me about my mother's funeral, she made me promise that if she died before I did, she was to be cremated and scattered, preferably over a lake on a windy day.

"If there is any soul left in the shell, and I don't believe there is, I don't want mine trapped underground. I want it out there, free, floating around."

"Here we go," I took her arm. "Just take a couple of deep breaths. We'll be back out before you know it."

Our visit went pretty much as we expected. Hushed voices, muted organ music and the cloying smell of too many flowers. There were three rooms, each with a sign bearing the family name and a little logo of the funeral home. Maybe Helen has a point, I thought.

The Menard family was represented by a slightly worn version of Gerry. Same sandy-coloured hair, same large bone structure, maybe five or so years older. There was no casket, just a picture of the deceased in front of a large spray of gladioli. Alone in the room, Gerry's brother was soft-spoken and polite when we went in but turned a little frosty when we introduced ourselves as being from Rosewood. We muttered the usual, banal words that don't really do anything for anyone, signed a little card for a donation to the local AIDS hospice and hightailed it out of the room.

"One down, one to go," Helen whispered. We linked arms and walked along the foyer to the next room. She was so tense I could have jabbed her arm with a knitting needle and not broken the skin.

A light snow was falling as we drove back across town. The moon was so bright and full, I switched off the headlights for a couple of miles on the backroad to the house, and the Chevy just glided quietly along like a ghost car.

"There now, that wasn't so bad, was it?" I asked.

"It was fucking awful," she said.

She was huddled in the corner of the passenger seat, wrapped in the old afghan I keep in the car.

"Yeah, well, at least we've done our duty. But I had a real problem in the so-called Haggerty Room. Just watching Mr. Dan 'Smarmy' Haggerty almost did me in—'so nice of you to come…I really appreciate it…poor Cathy would be so pleased…'" My hands tightened on the steering wheel. "Can you believe the gall? I was hard put not to slap him alongside the head. I wonder what all those friends and relatives in there would say if they knew he was doing the light fandango with another woman."

"I noticed quite a few of the signatures in the book were from Rosewood tenants," Helen said. "Cathy sure was well liked around the mall. There were quite a few people there, weren't there? Certainly a lot more than in Gerry's room."

"Two would have been more than Gerry had. I wonder why? I know we didn't like him, but surely somebody did. Kinda sad, isn't it? And that brother, in there alone. You'd think somebody would be keeping him company."

"Well, we're not going back to do it, Jenny, so just keep driving." She pulled the afghan a little tighter. "At least it's done now. Rosewood has been represented, and you were quite right, it certainly was a distraction. I haven't had such a good time since we went to that male strip joint last year. The one Shirley talked us into. 'Just like the Chippendales', she said."

"You mean the one where the guys on stage did strange things with onion rings?"

"Strange to folks like us, yeah."

We drove the last mile or so in silence, each to her own thoughts, the only sound the soft back-and-forth slurp of the windshield wipers.

"Ain't life strange, Jen?" Helen broke the silence.

"What d'you mean?"

"Well, somebody at that table wasn't meant to die." Back to the present. "I mean, except for maybe Jones Jr. and Menard, the three of them had nothing in common, did they? Just sharing a table, that's all. People do it all the time. See a spot and grab it."

She fell quiet again.

"I guess," I said. "But, you know, whoever pulled the trigger was aiming at one of them, that's for sure, and I, personally, have a hard job thinking it was Cathy."

I pulled into the driveway and turned off the engine.

"You still going to that wool place on Saturday?"

"I'm planning on it, but now the Jones boy is dead, I have to find out what's happening about his burial. We really need to present a united front on that one. All of us have to be there. Why? You change your mind about coming? We could take the pups to the wool place."

"You know, I just might. We'll see."

Eighteen

The twins spent the night on my bed. They'd started snuffling and snorting and charging around the mattress around three in the morning. Trying to stop them was as effective as nailing jelly on a wall. They simply thought my shouting and flailing arms were all part of a new game they'd invented and charged even harder. They won, of course, and I ended up with both of them bouncing from my head to my stomach and back again. The object now seemed to be who could lick me to death the fastest.

You'll pay for this, Helen, I thought, shoving them off me for the umpteenth time. Don't think you won't.

It took about half an hour for them to fall asleep and another ten seconds for me to join them, but drifting off, I had to admit there was something nice about having two cuddly, warm bodies snuggled against me.

The next time I woke up it was to the smell of bacon frying. I trekked through to the kitchen, followed closely by Eb and Neb, as I'd decided to call them, who were charging my ankles this time.

"You have a good night's sleep, Helen?"

The table was set, the kettle was boiling, and two cereal bowls full of puppy chow sat on the floor over by the sink. Our roasting pan, half-filled with water, was next to them. The old clock above the fireplace chimed once to signal seven-thirty.

"I've already been out for a run." She opened the back door and out went the dogs. "I was gonna take the pups, but they looked so comfortable in your bed, I didn't have the heart to wake them up."

"Don't worry about it. Tomorrow you can just lift them up when you get out of your bed, 'cause that's where they'll be." I poured a large cup of tea. "Or, better yet, they can spend the night in the kitchen. We'll rope them off an area. Last night was okay once, but I'm not doing it again."

We all ate in relative silence. At least, Helen and I did. The dogs, back inside and covered with snow, were attacking the cereal bowls with the same enthusiasm they'd used on my mattress. By now most of the kibble was on the floor, which was getting a wash into the bargain. Helen grabbed them just as they were about to leap into the roasting pan.

"Healthy appetites, at least," I said.

"I was thinking…"

"Do I want to hear this?" I interrupted.

"…instead of going with you tomorrow, I'll take these two over to the animal hospital. Get them checked and make arrangements to have their shots done."

"Sounds fair to me," I said. "'Specially as we don't know anything about them, or where they came from. If they were dumped, then I think the chances are good that nothing's been done up to now. You cover it off, and I'll give you a cheque for my half later on."

I pushed my plate away and took a last mouthful of tea. "What're we gonna do about them when we leave for work?"

Helen got up and started to clear the table. She was already dressed in her gray slacks and white shirt. "I thought I'd take them with me," she said. "They can bounce around the maintenance yard. It's fenced, and maybe I can get Ed to rig something up. Make them a little run or something."

"Oh, he's gonna love that," I said. "I'm sure he won't mind a bit."

"Jenny, it's too early for sarcasm. And anyway, it's only for a day or two. Just till they get used to their new home. When they're a little older, they can stay home. I just think it's a shame to leave them in a strange place right away."

"It obviously didn't bother whoever abandoned them yesterday," I said. "But, you're right, I can't stand the thought of them making hay in here while we're gone. God knows what we'd come home to. Take them to work. Maybe they'll earn their keep. You know, like watchdogs or something. Or maybe Shirley can get them working the photocopier."

I stood up and headed back up the hall. "I'm gonna have a shower. You can see to all this stuff, since I did the night shift. See you at work later."

•

Everything at Rosewood was reasonably normal, but then it usually is early in the morning before the phone starts ringing and the day starts pecking. I did a quick walkabout, grinning as I passed the stores which had been locked up yesterday. They were, of course, open for business, having paid up as we knew they would. The only hold-out was Santillo, and I was kind of hoping he'd keep sleeping in his store until Bob got back. I wanted to be there when that exchange took place. There was no doubt who'd win, but the conversation was sure to be educational, and I'm always willing to learn something new, figuring that whatever you learn is never a disadvantage.

Upstairs, Shirley had flipped the phones down to the Info Booth, and she was working away on her computer, fingers flying at somewhere around Mach Two.

"What are you up to this morning?" I asked.

"Just getting all these reports ready for Head Office. Bob left a pile of stuff the other day, and it has to be down there this aft." She hit the print button and swung around. "Another couple of hours, and I'm done. Was there something you wanted, Jenny?"

"Not really. Just saying hello. I do have some news though…"

"Oh, you mean the dogs. How'd they spend the night?"

"God save Ireland, Shirley, is there anything you don't know before I do?"

"Not a lot. By the by, the scoop on the Jones funeral is on your desk. I sent flowers. The boys' paycheques are there as well. So's your mail, Charlie wants to see you and the strawberry people are delighted that you're gonna be a judge." She swung back around and started pounding the keyboard with a vengeance. "The Santa suits are in your office. They don't fit. You're to call Tiny and, at some point today, Phillip Shawson wants a statement faxed about your original conversation with Dick Simmons. When you want your calls, check down at the booth. That's it for now."

I was dismissed.

Phillip Shawson is our company lawyer, so I guess the threatened lawsuit was going ahead or, at least, they were preparing for it. Simmons didn't have a hope in hell of getting any kind of settlement from Shawson, in court or out of it. The owners of Rosewood have a singular policy—don't pay out money, take it in—and you'd have to walk a lot of miles to get the better of Shawson, a fancy Philadelphia lawyer if ever there was one.

Putting first things first, I called a local woman who'd done some sewing for me in the past and made arrangements for Tiny to go see her and get measured up for two new Santa suits.

"Do you want me to get the material, Jenny?" she asked.

"I'd appreciate it. It'll save me some time, and you know better what you need. I'll call downstairs to the fabric outlet and speak to the manager. Just pick what you want and he'll bill me directly. Thanks, Kathy. I'll give Tiny your number, and he'll call you about a time."

Blessed with pretty good recall, I typed out an almost verbatim report on my Saturday meeting with Dick Simmons as the next order of business and faxed it off to Shawson's office, adding Hobart's name and the cop shop phone number in case they wanted details of his interview with the gentleman.

A quick glance at a scribbled note in Shirley's usually neat handwriting showed that Stephen Jones Jr. was resting at the Simpson and Bowler Funeral Home downtown. The visiting hours were listed, donations to the children's wing of the hospital were requested in lieu of flowers and the funeral service was to be held on Monday, November 9 at 11 a.m., followed by a private, family only, internment. Seemed awfully rushed to me. Maybe the Councillor thought his wife had been through enough already without dragging it out any more or, who knows, maybe it was a religious thing.

I picked up the note, added one of my own to Bob saying that we should all arrange to be at the funeral, grabbed the boys' paycheques and went up the hall to the front office.

"Shirley, I'm just going out to see what Charlie wants, and I'll get the second signature on these cheques while I'm at it." I dropped the note about Jones on her desk. "Make sure Bob gets this when you're playing catch up with him on Monday, will you? Just in case I forget or I'm not here. You might make a photocopy for Keith, and I'll tell Helen."

She didn't even look up, just nodded and waved a hand in my general direction.

•

Charlie and his crew had just about finished the upper level. I had to hand it to the Biker Boys. They might look a bit to the left of centre, but they sure knew their job.

"Looks good, Charlie." I watched as he put the finishing touches on a piece of garland round the base of a lantern and signalled to one of his guys to switch on the light. The flame-shaped bulb came alive, and its reflection caught and sparkled in the red and silver berries of the garland.

"Thanks, Jenny." He climbed down and dusted his hands on the seat of his jeans. "We're almost done up here. Another coupla days, and this old popsicle stand'll be ready for Santa."

"Shirley said you wanted to see me."

"Yeah, something's come up. I've been called to another site that's having a coupla problems with their electrical system. Seems the flickering lights won't flicker, and the static ones keep going on and off."

"What are you telling me, Charlie?"

"Just that I'm not gonna be here for the rest of today, and possibly some part of tomorrow. Doesn't sound too serious, so I should have it fixed in a jiff. Maybe even by tonight."

"And…?"

"And I'm leaving the boys here. They pretty much know what's next anyway, but I didn't want to be AWOL if you came looking for me."

"And I'm to deal with the Standing Stones by myself?"

"Now, Jenny, you'll be fine. They've got the schedule. Just

go over it with them a couple of times. Make sure you're all on the same wavelength. 'Sides, they like you. One of them's in love with your hair. Says it reminds him of an Irish setter they had when he was a kid."

"Oh, well then…" I glanced over at the guys. One of them was grinning at me and nudging the giant beside him. "Hurry back, Charlie."

I took off in search of Evans, the department store manager, got the boys' cheques signed and made my way downstairs and outside to the maintenance yard to check on my children. They were wrapped around each other and sound asleep on what appeared to be a man's work parka, complete with fur trim. A plastic gallon jug had been cut down to hold a mound of kibble and another was filled with water. There were two green tennis balls and a teddy bear lying just to the left of the parka. Good old Ed. I might have known he'd spoil them immediately, after he'd grouched at Helen for the required amount of time.

Back inside, I went over to the Information Booth. "Any calls for me, Mary?"

"Keith was just here, and I gave them to him. He was on his way back upstairs."

"Thanks." I handed her Kathy's number. "Get hold of Tiny in Maintenance and give him this, would you? Tell him to call her and get over to be measured for the Santa suits. He's to do it today. She's only got a week to get them ready, and that's a lot of sewing."

"You taking calls up there now?"

"Give it another hour or so. Shirley'll buzz you."

•

Helen and Keith were just going into Bob's office when I got upstairs. Shirley wasn't at her desk, and Keith waved me in and closed the door. They stayed standing, and both of them looked pretty pleased about something. Helen had her coat on and was pulling a pair of gloves out of a pocket.

"What's up, you two? Somebody else not paying their rent?"

"Better than that, Jenny. Hard to believe, but better than that," Keith said. "Tell her, Helen."

"Our troubles could be over, Jenny," she said. "Looks like the cops are about to make an arrest."

I plopped into the nearest chair and stared at her. This was indeed a bombshell of the first order.

"Who?" I finally got out.

"They picked Haggerty up this morning and took him back in for more questioning. Bartolo just called. He seems to think this could be it. I'm on my way over there now."

"But how…what about…?"

She shook her head and walked over to open Bob's escape door.

"Don't ask, Jenny, 'cause I don't know," she said. "The minute I do, I'll be back. It could be a while," she added, over her shoulder, "so you see to the dogs."

Keith sat down, and we just looked at each other.

"I'm stunned," I said. "Absolutely stunned. After all this performance, can it be this easy?"

"I know. So am I. It's classic, though, isn't it?"

"Classic?"

"Well, you hear it all the time. The husband strays, the wife finds out, she's the one with the money. That kind of thing."

"I guess," I said. "But with Menard's background and rumours of drug dealers, gay lovers, et cetera, et cetera, and throw in his and the Jones kid's connection, if there really was one, to the shoplifting ring and/or the prostitution business—makes it hard to believe it's as straightforward as a husband killing his wife over another woman."

"They say most murders are committed over love or money. Sure seems to prove the truth of that theory."

I shook my head, still having a problem with it. "But Cathy was just an ordinary little woman running an ordinary little wool shop. And God knows, from what I've seen, the scarlet woman is no oil painting, plus Dan Haggerty's got the personality of a piece of cod. And to think I shook his hand at the funeral home last night."

I got up and started pacing around the office. "It's just not right. I'm telling you, Keith, it's not right. Think about it for a minute. Three people dead because that asshole couldn't keep his fucking zipper closed."

Keith got up and opened the door. "C'mon, Jenny. I'll buy you a cup of tea. There's no use getting any more worked up. After all, he hasn't even been arrested yet."

We stopped and left a note for Shirley, who still wasn't at her desk. With her talent for getting hot-off-the-press info, she was probably over at the cop shop, sitting in on the interview.

"Besides," Keith continued, "I'd bet my shirt there's a lot more to this. I know little or nothing about the Haggertys and, other than buying wool from the wife, neither do you. You're just assuming she was an ordinary little woman."

That was Keith. Ever the voice of reason. The fact that he was right wasn't the point. Three people were still as dead as doorknobs.

Nineteen

Helen came back with the news that Dan Haggerty had indeed been arrested and charged with the murders. We were sitting in my office. She'd been back about an hour, and after a quick check on her Security people and making a shift change, came in to spill what little she knew—which wasn't much.

"What did George say?" I asked.

"Nada. He didn't come out of his office the whole time I was there," she said. "From the way he was glaring through the glass at Bartolo and Hobart, I guess he figured that one of them had called me and, with things the way they are between us right now, I'm sure he wasn't amused to see me there."

"What a shame. I'd hate George to be upset." I said.

She chugged back a swig of coffee, leaned back and put her feet on the desk.

"Anyway, I didn't learn much in the way of the dirty details. Just that the Haggertys, apparently, had some pretty heavy-duty insurance on each other and, when that information turned up, the boys checked his alibi a little closer. It didn't hold up."

"What was his alibi?" I held up my hand. "Don't tell me, let me guess. He was busy playing doctor and nurse with the jewellery dame."

"I don't know. All I know is it didn't compute, as they say. At least, that's the way Hobart put it."

"And…?" I asked.

"And nothing. His intercom buzzed, and the next thing I knew, I was sent packing. George, I guess. And after all the running back and forth I've done with this thing."

"But I don't understand what made them suspect him in the first place." I said. "I thought they were hot to trot with all these other leads. What you were saying the other night. Drugs, prostitution, that sort of stuff. What about all that? We were all so convinced that Menard was the target, and Cathy and the Jones' son just had the bad luck to be at that table. At least, that made a certain kind of sense, especially now we know about the father's extracurricular activities. People have affairs all the time that don't lead to murder. I could believe blackmail before I could believe the Haggerty bit.

"Well, it seemed the most obvious, so I guess that's where they started. But good investigators—and Hobart, Bartolo and George are three of the best—wouldn't assume anything, Jenny. They do their homework thoroughly, and I'm sure they were checking all the victims' backgrounds right from the get-go."

She handed me her empty cup and stood up. "Anyway, that's it for now. I'm sure I'll learn a bit more in the next day or so, if his lordship calms down any. Throw that out for me, would you? I'm off."

I walked up the hall with her.

"Bad timing, Helen. That's what this is, bad timing."

"What d'you mean?"

"Well, this isn't exactly the best time for you to be pissed off at George. Couldn't you get back on his good side for a while—get some pillow talk or something going—at least until we get the dope on Haggerty? I liked it better when you were on the 'inside'."

Helen put the brakes on. We were halfway up the hall

towards the Security office. "I can't believe you just said that."

"Now, don't get huffy. My mother always said 'fair exchange is no robbery' and, you must admit, it'd be nice to be privy to a daily report. And it is our business. It's our mall that was used for the dirty deed."

"Well, then, you call George and offer to bed him. See how that plays out," she said, walking away.

"Nasty, nasty," I called after her.

•

I took a spin around the mall to check how the decorations were going and sensed an undercurrent of excitement everywhere. News of the arrest had, naturally, made it over to Rosewood, and everyone was avid for details. After I'd been stopped a dozen times and pumped for information, I gave up and went back to hide in my office. Shirley, back at her desk with the phone clamped to her ear, handed me another pile of message slips. All the buttons on her phone were flashing.

"What d'you think, Jenny?" She hung up and ignored the next ring. "Good news, huh?"

"The best." I sat on the corner of her desk. "Now we can maybe get back to normal, if there is such a thing in this business." I shook my head. "But you know…"

"What?"

"Oh, nothing." I headed for my office, and she immediately got up and followed me.

"Oh, nothing…what?"

"It just doesn't feel right, Shirley. That's all."

"But why?"

"That's the problem. I don't know why. I just know it doesn't." I gave myself a mental shake. "You'd better get a memo out around the mall. It's getting so a person can't go two steps without being stopped. Give them our official line."

"And just what would that be?" she asked.

"Say the police have made an arrest, and any further information will come from them. Get Keith to sign it, and ask Helen to give you a couple of her people to deliver it. I want to make sure it gets to every store."

"Won't stop the talk." She closed the door, lifted up her skirt and started straightening her pantyhose. Her colour for today was buttercup yellow, head to toe. I wondered, not for the first time, how she managed to get the exact shades in tops and bottoms, not to mention shoes.

"I know, but it may cut down on the questions, and it just might stop your phone ringing off the hook." I watched her contortions for a minute. "What are you doing, Shirley?"

"It's these damn one-size-fits-all pantyhose," she said. "Last pair I bought, I could've pulled up around my neck with a drawstring." She lowered her skirt and smoothed it out. "The crotch on these ones travels up and down between my knees and my whatsit. Anyway, one of the phone calls was Ed. He wants to know which one of you ladies is going down to poop and scoop after your dogs. He's left a water hose out as well, so you can wash down the yard."

"I'll call him."

"He's gone for the day." She fished around in her skirt pocket. "And I'm about to be off, too. But here's the key to the fence gate. He left it for you."

"Thanks, Shirley. How d'you feel about making a pass through the yard on your way out?"

"I've got enough clean-up waiting for me at home. I'm gonna see to this memo and then get going. I'll lock the outer door so you're not disturbed. See you Monday morning when you get back from the funeral."

Shirley's a widow with three teenagers who, from what I've gathered over the years, do absolutely squat around the house. For somebody who's so organized at work, I can't figure out why she lets them away with it. Good, old, unconditional mother-love, I guess. Or maybe emotional guilt about the absence of a father. Who knows? I'd been brought up with a mother's love, too, but it had never meant getting away with murder.

I plonked down in my chair, thinking "I've done it again." How come I've never realized before how many expressions have to do with death? And how come I know so many of them?

Shuffling through the messages, I saw they could all wait for Monday. Today had been a corker. I was tired and it was kind of late to be returning phone calls. Nobody ever wants to talk about anything meaningful last thing on a Friday, and most of the calls were from tenants. Probably wanting more dirt about the arrest.

The last one was a handwritten note from Tiny saying he'd noticed, in the hospital parking lot the other night, that my car radio wasn't working, so he'd spent some time on it and the broken lock on the driver's side this afternoon, and it was "A-okay" now. What a guy! I really had misjudged him at first. The note finished with a little arrow in the bottom right hand corner. I turned the paper over, where he'd added that he was being fitted tomorrow for his Santa suits, and he liked the pups almost as much as he liked the Chevy.

Contrary to what I'd said to Helen, the timing of Haggerty's arrest couldn't be more perfect. Next Saturday was our big parade. The heavy portion of our radio ads with the new jingle started tomorrow and continued through the week. A Christmas flyer was going out on Tuesday, and there was a scheduled double-page spread in next week's paper. And, as if on cue, the shootings had been cleared up, although there was still something niggling at me about the whole thing. I didn't have a name for it, but it wouldn't go away. It all seemed too pat—insurance money, lover, wife in the way. There was more to this, but what?

•

Getting ready to leave, I pinned a note on the wall to phone Hobart tomorrow and invite him and his partner to lunch one day next week and another one to set up a Christmas lunch with Barb Donaldson or perhaps invite her to a ringside seat at the parade. It would make up for being so abrupt with her, even though she'd asked for it. The murders notwithstanding, it was time to get the Christmas spirit going. Maybe I'd call Jim as well.

I picked up the radio and told Helen I was on my way home, and I'd take the pups with me.

"You want me to pick up some deli stuff?" she asked. "I'll be about another hour or so. By the way, Tiny cleaned up after the dogs. Said they were no trouble at all. Is this guy too good to be true or what?"

"A prince. See you at home."

Twenty

Saturday morning came early, and, for the second day in a row, I wasn't alone in the bed. Eb and Neb were up to their usual antics, jumping back and forth from the pillow to my chest, poking me in the face with cold, wet noses. I shoved them onto the floor and looked at the clock. Quarter to seven.

"Look here, guys, it's Saturday. Give it a break. Go find your other mother."

I rolled over so I couldn't see their eyes, but that didn't work either. They simply charged the bed with flying leaps until they finally got a pawhold, scrambled up the side and we were at it again. I gave up, just as they wanted, got out of bed and we all traipsed through to the kitchen. I booted them out the door to pee then fixed a pot of tea and plugged in the toaster.

Standing by the counter, I looked over at our latest contraption—a large wire cage which Helen had come through the door with last night.

"And just what is that supposed to be?" I had watched her manhandle it across the room.

"I got it at the pet store. They're for training dogs. You put your pet in it whenever you go out and have to leave it alone. The premise is that they won't soil where they sleep, so it trains them to wait till you get home." She'd put her hands on her hips and surveyed her purchase. "What d'you think?"

I'd looked at her, at the cage then at the pups.

"I'll take it back tomorrow," she said.

•

The doggies were head-butting the door to get back in when Helen came downstairs, hair at sixes-and-sevens and the jacket on her flannelette pyjamas all twisted off to one side. A vision of loveliness.

"What's all the noise?" She felt her way over to the coffeepot. "I was trying to sleep. It's Saturday, you know."

"Don't." I let the dogs in and put down their breakfast and popped two slices of bread in the toaster.

"You want a couple of poached eggs?" I asked. "Or some kibble?"

"No, thanks. It's too early." This from the health freak in the family. "What time're you going to that wool place? I thought it was only a couple hours drive?"

"Changed up my mind, as my sister used to say." I put my eggs in the nuker and set the timer for two minutes. "I'm going tomorrow instead."

"You've been waiting all week for today to arrive and I swear, if you don't start knitting again soon, I'll go nuts watching your hands fidget."

The timer on the microwave went off, sending the dogs into a frenzy, but at least it was Helen they dove for this time. She picked them up and buried her face in their fur.

"Remember I told you that Tiny quietly fixed the radio in my car yesterday?" I set my breakfast down and tucked in. "So, since he likes the car so much, and he was good enough to fix it on his own bat, I thought I'd phone and ask if he'd like to come with me. Even let him drive."

"Boy, that really is an offer. Brando couldn't have come up with a better one." Her eyes were open all the way now she'd finished her first cup of coffee. "Seems I'm hearing Tiny's name quite a bit now, Jenny. Maybe you should take a closer look at him and forget Jim."

"Nice segue, Helen, but we're not going there right now. To get back to what I was saying, between his father and his job, I don't think he goes to too many places just for the hell of going."

"How is his father?"

"Actually, he's home and doing pretty well, from what I gather. Tiny managed to make arrangements through one of those community groups for some part-time, volunteer home care, so things are looking up a little."

"But that doesn't answer my first question. Why aren't you going today?"

"Tiny's got a fitting for his Santa suits. Kathy's making two new ones, and I'm sure not gonna screw that up. Besides, I've got a few odds and ends to clean up at work, so I'll go in for a couple of hours while you're at the vet's."

The phone rang and Helen got up to answer it, said "hello" a number of times and then hung up.

"That's the fourth time since last night," she said. "I tried that 'last call' gizmo we've got, but it just says the number's not available. Strange."

We left the house together about ten-thirty. Packing Helen's station wagon was a bit of a pickle, to say the least. We finally managed to get the cage on the back seat and the pups into the back of the car. They'd probably roll around a bit, but that was better than attacking Helen while she was driving.

"Sure you can manage?" I asked. "I'll come, too, if you like. Hold on to them."

"No, I'll be fine, Jenny. They've got to get used to it, so they may as well start now."

When I got to the office, I called Tiny at home. He was thrilled with my offer but turned me down.

"Sorry, Jenny. Appreciate the invite, but Dad's not feeling too great, so I don't want to be out more than I have to this weekend. Sure would love a raincheck though and, if it wouldn't be a lot of trouble, Dad would be thrilled if you'd let him come for a drive one day, too. He used to have a twin to your car. Loved it."

"Of course I'll take him out, and I'm sorry you can't make it tomorrow. Tell you what—next Saturday's the parade, as you know. How about we switch cars on Friday and you bring your Dad with you in the Chevy early Saturday when you're coming to get ready for your starring role? It can be the car's last run for this year."

"You mean that, Jenny?"

"Of course. And I'll also make sure he gets a ringside seat for the parade."

"No shit."

"Tiny…"

He laughed. "Gotcha."

•

My paperwork only took a couple of hours. It consisted of making a pile of notes about things to be checked for the January Sidewalk Sale to make sure all was in order.

I knew once the Christmas season really kicked off, I'd want to sit back and enjoy. The only problems would be Santa-related and, hopefully, not too many of them. Another note went up on the board as a reminder to make up a little bonus cheque for each of the boys. They had certainly performed over and above their job descriptions and besides, they were nice kids.

By one o'clock, I was done. The office was quiet, no phones ringing, no radios crackling—nothing at all like last Saturday. I sat for a while, thinking back to Ugly Bug Simmons and everything that had come after. Had it really only been a week ago? Amazing what can happen in the span of seven short days.

I fished out the piece of paper with the wool farm address and got a phone number from the operator. The call was picked up on the first ring and a deep, cultured voice announced, "Delurey Wools, Robert Delurey speaking."

I introduced myself, explained my problem with the new green colour and was told that indeed their store—on the farm property—would be open tomorrow, and I was more than welcome to "pay us a visit." He went on to give me explicit directions, told me to drive safely and then excused himself as "I have a lamb to feed." That done, I put on my coat, picked up my purse and headed up the hall, swinging the outer door open.

My mother stood in the doorway, shrouded in black.

"Oh, Jesus," My breath left with a swoosh, and I dropped my bag, one hand clawing at the panelling behind me.

The tiny figure stepped through the door and a thin, almost transparent hand touched my arm.

"Ms. Turnbull?" It was like being brushed by a feather, so soft were both the touch and the voice. "I'm so sorry. Did I startle you?"

Still fighting for air, I leaned my head against the wall and closed my eyes for a second or two.

"I was just about to knock," she said, "when you opened the door. May I come in?"

"Please…" I made some of kind of motion, I think, towards the couch, still not quite able to shake my mother's image loose. "Just give me a minute. You were someone else…I mean, I thought you were someone else."

I pointed at the couch again and she lowered herself with minimum movement onto the edge of the middle cushion. Still quivering, I took the chair behind Shirley's desk.

"What can I do for you, Mrs.…?"

"Jones," she said, "Eulah Jones."

She lifted her mourning veil very gently over the brim of a small, black pillbox hat, revealing a face whose eyes were of such pale blue, they heightened the transparent look of her skin. Dressed completely in black, from hat to shoes, and probably not more than ninety pounds, she was the very antithesis of her husband. She returned her hands to her lap, both of them ringless and one of them clutching a pair of black kid gloves which she started to twist.

Each of us spoke at the same time.

"Mrs. Jones…"

"Ms. Turnbull…"

I got up and moved around the desk to sit in the armchair beside her.

"Mrs. Jones, I'm so terribly sorry about the loss of your son. We all are. I can't begin to imagine the extent of your grief and, on behalf of Rosewood…"

She leaned forward to put a hand on my knee and gave a small, sad smile. "Ms. Turnbull…"

"Jenny. Please."

"Thank you, that's very kind." She drew in a breath, took her hand back and looked down at her lap. "Most people have been very kind."

Out came a linen handkerchief which she used to dab at

her eyes. Watching her was painful.

"Mrs. Jones, why don't I make us both a nice cup of tea? I'm sure being here can't be easy for you." I got up and went to the kitchen, saying over my shoulder. "You just take a few moments."

I patted my face all over with cold water and took my time setting up a tea tray. What the hell was she doing here? By the time I got back to the reception area, she seemed quite composed. Thank God, I thought, I can't handle this if she gets weepy. I busied myself pouring tea and offering cookies.

"Who did you think I was, Jenny? When I first came in. You looked quite taken aback."

"Oh, that was stupid," I said. "You'll have to forgive me, I was just startled for a minute."

"It was more than that," she said. "I upset you."

"It wasn't you, it's just…" my turn to feel for a hanky "…you look remarkably like my mother, and just for an instant…a flash, you understand…I thought she was standing there. Silly of me. She's been gone for some years now."

"I can tell you miss her very much."

"I still talk to her all the time."

She picked up her cup and sipped at the contents with hardly a movement of her lips. How on earth did this woman ever end up married to Stephen Jones, let alone bear him a son? She looked far too fragile to cope with those two and all their doings.

"That's nice. I always wanted a daughter," she said. "But Stephen, my husband, decided after our son was born, that one child was enough. He adored little Stephen, you know." A little sigh escaped the colourless lips. "I've always regretted his decision, but I'm sure you're aware how forceful his personality is." Another soft sigh.

"Of course, I did what he wanted." She looked somewhere off in the distance for a bit, then added, quietly, so quietly, "So now we don't have any."

I couldn't think of a thing to say that didn't sound trite. I mean, how would "there, there, things'll get better" sound, when any idiot knew they wouldn't? I wanted, desperately, to hug her, but settled for gesturing with the teapot instead.

"Thank you, but no." She got to her feet slowly, but determinedly. "You've been very gracious, but I really must leave now. My husband would be furious if he knew I was here, in this building, let alone in your office. But I imagine you know that." We walked to the door, and the veil was adjusted back down over her face. "I came by your office on the off-chance you'd be here. I just wanted to thank you for the flowers and your very kind note." The soft fingers touched my arm again, briefly this time, and she paused at the door. "And I wanted to spend a few minutes in the place where my son died. I killed him, you know."

"Mrs. Jones…" This was pitiful. What the hell was this woman doing out of the hospital? "Please don't…"

"It's true. I should have been a better mother, Jenny. Stephen, my husband, always said I was far too lenient with the boy, never able to discipline myself, so how could I expect to discipline our son?"

She pulled on her gloves, smoothing them down, one finger at a time, as if struck by past memories and then, so quietly I almost didn't hear her, "He's always so angry."

"Mrs. Jones, I'm about to leave too. Can I give you a drive home?"

"No, thank you, Jenny. I have my car." That wan, little smile again.

"But…"

"I'll be fine on my own. Really. I'd rather be alone. I'm quite used to it. I've done what I came to do, and now it just remains to be with my son on Monday. For the burial, you know. The final act that we're all faced with, eventually."

She touched my arm again. Even gloved, the fingers had no substance.

"And please don't feel obliged to attend, Jenny. We've had our talk, and I think it might be better if…Stephen, you know…" Her voice trailed off and, with a last, little pat, she moved away.

I stood in the doorway, tears dripping off my chin, and watched the sad little figure walk up the hall and turn left by the exit sign.

•

I was in the kitchen rinsing the tea things when I heard the outer door open again.

"I'll be right there," I called, wiping my hands and hurrying out. "Did you forget something?"

Jim was standing beside Shirley's desk.

"What are you doing here?" I could barely get the words out.

"I came to talk to you. There's something we need to straighten out." He held out both hands and then dropped them.

"What?"

"Do you think we could at least sit down, Jenny?" He leaned forward and looked a little closer at my face. "What's wrong with you?"

"D'you mean what's wrong with me overall, or what's wrong because I got soap in my eyes from the sink and they're watering?" I sank onto the couch, and he sat down in the chair beside it. "What did you want to say? An apology, perhaps?"

He gave a short laugh. "Not exactly. I want to talk about our relationship."

"Professional or personal?"

He inched a little closer, and I got up and moved to Shirley's chair.

"I can see, for some reason known only to you, Jenny, this isn't exactly a good time, but I'm here now, and I'd like to say my piece." He cleared his throat and sat up a little straighter. "We've been seeing each other for a few months now and seem to be generally compatible in our likes and dislikes, but your tantrum last week, over a bit of liver…"

"Jim, stop with the preamble. Just exactly what, and I mean exactly, is the point you're trying to make here? I'm in no mood for a magnum opus, so for God's sake, spit it out and keep it short."

"As you like." He got up and smoothed down the front of his shirt. "We're done."

I sagged back in the chair. "See, there you go again. We're done talking? Or we're done with our relationship? You're done with me? Or I'm done with you?"

"I've thought a lot about this in the past few days, and I believe it's best if our involvement is a purely professional one starting today." He walked over and stood in the doorway. "Obviously, with the mood you're in, it'd be better if we just end this conversation right now. Sometimes, the least said, the soonest mended and that way, perhaps we can at least continue to be civil."

"I'll work on that. Meanwhile, shut the door behind you."

Twenty-One

"I'm telling you, Helen, it was fuckin' awful."

"I thought you were almost ready to end that relationship anyway. Maybe it's just bothering you that he did it for you."

We were just finishing dinner, two huge logs were crackling away in the fireplace, and the pups lay on an old rug on the hearth. They were pretty subdued from their visit to the vet.

"I'm not talking about Jim. That's actually a relief, I guess, though you're right, it's a blow to the ego when the other person scoops you first. No, I'm talking about Eulah Jones. In all my born days, I've never seen such a pathetic figure. "Look." I held out an arm and pushed up my sweater sleeve. "Goosebumps. I'm still chilled."

"Doesn't sound like she's had the happiest of lives," Helen said. "What a waste. And imagine feeling responsible for the death of your own son. I used to believe that everybody ultimately chose their own lifestyle, but I don't know any more if that's true."

I got up and poked the fire a bit and sat in the rocker, hugging both arms across my chest.

"Well, this afternoon certainly made a good case for the single life, as far as I'm concerned. When I think of that poor woman and the years she's spent with his honour, the councillor—years she'll never get back. Why didn't she leave him a long time ago? That's what I can't fathom. I'd have dropped him like a brick."

"That probably wouldn't have been an option for her," Helen said. "People of her generation—once married—stayed married, and I'll bet even if the thought had entered her head, she'd dismiss it pretty quick. And not to be unkind, there's a certain status for her, being married to a relatively big fish in a little pond."

"Too bad fish can't drown," I said. "To think I was actually feeling sorry for him a couple of days ago. Bastard."

Helen got up and went to our supply cupboard beside the fridge.

"Go and put on your snuggly nightie and bedsock ensemble. I'll pour us a little brandy, and we'll change the subject. Talk about something more pleasant. Eulah Jones' life isn't your problem, and you certainly can't do anything for her now. Besides, I'm sure she has her own way of dealing with her husband. She's been married to him long enough."

"Talking about pleasant," I said, getting up, "what's happening about Haggerty and the murder charges?"

"Now," she said, "that's pretty interesting. I had lunch with George…"

My eyebrows went up as my stomach sank.

"…no, Jenny. I wanted to clear the air, that's all. Tell him I'm with the status quo, but would like us to stay friends. Maybe even still date once in a while."

"Bet he just loved that," I said.

"Well, it's free sex and no commitment," she said. "How can you hate it? There's nothing wrong with my libido, you know."

"Get back to Haggerty, Helen. What's 'pretty interesting'?"

She came over with the brandy snifters, and I sat back down.

"George isn't quite happy with the arrest. Says it doesn't feel exactly right to him."

"Now that is interesting, because I've had the same feeling for the past couple of days," I said, loud enough to make the dogs stir. "But if that's what he thinks, why the hell did they arrest Haggerty?"

"I guess there was a push on from his Chief, and there's certainly enough evidence, together with no alibi, to charge him."

"What George's problem then?"

"No problem. Just instinct. But when you've been a cop as long as George, instinct's a pretty powerful thing. Anyway..." she got up and picked up one of the still-sleeping pups, "...nothing's changed. He's just not happy about the situation."

"Neither am I, but when you think about, it does seem to fit what Keith called a classic pattern. The insurance money and his adultery and all. Still, I dunno..."

"What?" she asked.

"Doesn't blasting away in a crowded mall seem a bit overdone for a man trying to kill his wife? You'd think he..."

"Don't think, Jenny, just leave it to George."

I finished my drink and went over to the door to peer outside. The backyard had a deeper layer of snow than earlier on and the Chevy, which I hadn't bothered to put in the garage, was wearing a coat of it.

Helen, still holding the dogs, headed for the back stairs.

"You want to watch a movie?" I asked.

"Nope," she said. "I'm going to run a tub and soak for a while. Be back down later to help you clean up. Just leave everything the way it is."

"I'll do it." I went to the sink and ran the taps. "After today, I need something mindless to do. There's only so much a person can take, and I'm there already. Look in my bathroom before you go up. I bought some new green apple bath oil. Help yourself."

I washed and dried the dinner things and put them away, then swept the floor and tidied the counter tops. Eulah Jones followed me around the room like a shadow. I couldn't shake her loose. Probably, if she hadn't been so like my mother, if only in looks, she'd be easier to dismiss.

I fished out my knitting bag, checked that the sweater pattern was in it and set it ready on the counter near the door so I wouldn't forget it in the morning. Helen came down the stairs just as I was tamping down the logs.

"Not watching the movie?"

"Changed my mind," I said. "I'm planning an early start tomorrow, so I'm about to go to bed. Boy, Helen, if ever I needed a long drive to clear away the blues, it's now. Think of it—two hours each way with nothing pecking at me, and I've even got a radio that works. If it wasn't stupid, I'd leave right now."

"Go to bed, Jenny. And don't make any noise in the morning."

Twenty-Two

An hour north of home, the landscape took on the look of a pastoral Christmas card scene. Snow-covered fields gave way every few miles to snow-covered pine trees which, in turn, opened up now and again to show glimpses of houses and barns set back at the end of long driveways banked with ramrod straight rows of trees planted as windbreaks. I fished around in my purse for my cell phone to call home and tell Helen what she was missing. No luck. I must have left it in the kitchen.

It was all quite beautiful, but much as I loved being here on this particular morning on this particular day, it wasn't for me. I'm a concrete jungle kid who gets a nosebleed if I have to leave the city for any length of time. However, I did need that wool, even more than I needed a day to myself. I cranked up the radio just as Tom Jones finished belting out "Forgive me, Delilah, I just couldn't take any more."

"Good thinking, Tommy," I said out loud. "Neither can I. Time for breakfast."

Another few miles produced a green and white road sign, one with international symbols that you've passed before you figure them out, but I did spot a knife, fork and plate, so I swung off at the next exit and, a few hundred yards along, pulled into the parking lot of "Pop's Place". I drove around two islands of gas pumps and stopped in front of a log structure whose window sign said "Best Food Anywhere!" An adjacent building, same logs, advertised "Best Rooms Anywhere!" Quite by chance, I'd arrived in Utopia.

Half-an-hour later, fortified by bacon, eggs and hashbrowns, I was back on the road with the gas tank topped up, and my directions to Delurey Wools confirmed by Pop himself.

"Sure, I know Bob and Anne," he said. "They eat here every Friday."

"Fish Friday?" I asked.

"Nope. It's my Lamb Curry they come for. Matter of fact, it's their lamb. They provide the meat, I do the cooking."

I shuddered. That's another reason I'd never make a farmer's wife. Imagine eating something you'd known personally. Grabbing a couple of packs of meat in styrofoam trays at the supermarket provides a certain distance from thinking about something having to die so you can eat.

"Well, thanks for your help. And, by the way, breakfast was great."

"Glad you enjoyed it. Our own eggs. Got hens out the back." He turned back to the kitchen. "Have a great day, now. Stop in on your way back."

I was gone before he could say where he got the bacon.

After I turned off the highway at the "Delurey Wools" sign, a hard, packed-dirt road, thick with trees on either side, ran about five hundred yards straight then skewed left to open onto another Krieghoff painting.

A large, handsome, log house stood tall and proud just beyond a cleared parking area at the front of the property. Off to the left was a massive two-story wooden building with a herringbone pattern of bricks set into the façade. A wood-burned sign told me this was the "Wool Warehouse". At the back of the house, not too far away, stood the barn and a few other outbuildings. Everything was covered with a thick blanket of snow, and there wasn't a sheep to be seen.

I parked the Chevy, got out and headed for the warehouse, stopping midway as somebody behind me said, "Miss Turnbull, I presume?" Recognizing the same cultured tones of our telephone exchange, I turned around and held out my hand.

"Yes. And you're Mr. Delurey."

The man's physical presence was the embodiment of his voice, his home and his livelihood. Dressed in a chunky blue and white Nordic sweater and matching wool cap, he stood as tall and proud as the house behind him. A full beard, streaked with grey, matched the tight, curly hair poking out in all directions from under the cap. A lamb was cradled in the bend of one arm, and the only thing missing from the picture was a shepherd's crook.

"Welcome." He held out a hand. "How was your drive?"

"Exhilarating," I said. "I always love to get out into the countryside. Clears the cobwebs." I wasn't sure whether to pet the lamb or not. "Although I'm a bit leery of the weather. The snow's been getting a lot heavier for the last half hour."

The sharp, dark eyes travelled from my sweatshirt to slacks and down to the sneakers on my feet, but he made no comment. "Shall we go in?" Strong fingers gripped my elbow and steered me towards the house. "Anne is just making some hot chocolate."

Inside, we were met by two cats and a hulking, black dog of indeterminate breed with a motor-driven tail.

"Muffy, lie down now," said my host, as a pleasant voice called from off to the right.

"I'm in the kitchen. Come on through, I can't stop stirring."

I slipped off my shoes and Robert Delurey handed me a pair of knitted, thick woollen slippers. I loved this place already.

Anne Delurey stood by the stove tending to a pot of simmering chocolate. She, too, wore a heavy sweater, but hers was patterned with large flowers in glorious colours and topped an ankle length, soft brown skirt. A pair of slippers that matched mine peeped out from under the hem. Like her husband, I put her age somewhere in the early forties. She turned off the burner and poured the drink into three waiting mugs, added a dollop of whipped cream and set them on the kitchen table beside a plate of muffins.

Her voice, with its slight English accent, was as rich as her husband's, and her eyes held the same strong look of intelligence. "Robert told me about the problems you've been having at your shopping centre. He heard, of course, through our connection with the wool store. How awful for you."

I spooned some whipped cream up. "There has been arrest made, so things are turning around a bit. Getting back to almost normal. I guess you know Dan Haggerty?"

"Actually," she said, "we don't. We dealt with his wife, poor woman. What a terrible thing to have happened. A tragedy in the truest sense."

"A tragedy compounded by the senseless deaths of two others," I said.

From the look they exchanged, they obviously hadn't heard of the Jones boy's demise, so I briefly outlined the events of the last couple of days and ended with a plea not to talk about it any more, and to please call me Jenny.

"I'd really rather learn more about your operation here. I must say I'm very impressed." I looked around the large kitchen. "I've only been here a few minutes, and already it feels right."

"Thank you," Robert said. "I like to think of it as a Romance in the purest sense of the word. We started with half-a-dozen sheep and grew from there. Took quite a risk actually. That's why I bought six sheep in the first place, figuring if things didn't work out we could always eat them and, at least, we wouldn't starve. When we're finished our drinks, I'll lend you a pair of rubber boots and give you the grand tour, if you'd like."

"I'd love it." I finished off the last of my muffin and blew on the mug of chocolate. "I had the impression from Cathy that you'd been here for quite some time, but everything looks so new."

"We've actually been here for about fifteen years," Anne said, "but you're right, most of the house is quite new, and the warehouse just went up last spring. This kitchen is part of the original log cabin that stood on the farm in the late 1800s. We kept as much of the old structure as possible, and Robert simply built on to it."

"Are you a builder by trade, then?" I asked him.

They both laughed.

"I intended to be a teacher," he said, "as did Anne, but by the time I'd worked through my doctorate in philosophy, that went the way of all things. When Anne and I realized neither of us was happy, we just packed up and moved here."

"You make it sound deceptively simple," I said, "throwing caution to the winds."

"Of course it wasn't," Anne said. "But it came out all right in the end."

"Better than 'all right'," I said. "It's marvellous. How did you find this spot?"

"We used to come mushroom-hunting here in the summer," she said. "Robert did his thesis on mushrooms and their use in magic and rituals by the ancients. There are all sorts of folklore legends about fungi and their powers." She pointed to the window above the sink. "The second largest Faerie Ring in North America lies in that forest beyond the barn. So naturally, when the place went up for sale, we had to buy it."

"Faerie Ring?" I asked.

"Don't say you haven't heard of a Ring?" Robert shifted the lamb to his other arm. It was starting to make little crying sounds. He stood up and got a baby bottle full of milk from a pot on the stove. "With your heritage? I can't believe it."

"Believe it," I said. "I'm a transplanted Scot and didn't really live in Scotland very long. Obviously, not long enough for my education to include Faerie Rings."

He handed the lamb and bottle of milk to Anne. She cradled the animal and began feeding it, making soothing little noises.

"A Faerie Ring is an enchanted place—a magic place—inhabited by little folk who dance in its circle, a circle caused by ever-growing mushrooms. As they spread outwards, the grass darkens and forms a noticeable ring. The darkening is attributed, by legend, to the dancing."

"What a wonderful story," I said. "Now I'm really sorry it's snowing. I'd love to have seen it."

"It never snows inside the circle." He smiled and ducked his head. "But getting across the fields and through the trees is another matter."

He got up again and started to clear the table.

"It's a private place, and we normally don't show people where it is, but if you're truly interested and promise to keep it to yourself, I'll take you there next spring."

I finished up my chocolate, taking a last look around the room. I was sitting with a PhD, who was not only a wool farmer but an expert on mushrooms, giving me a talk on

Faerie Rings while his wife fed a lamb at the kitchen table. No wonder I felt so at home.

"Cross my heart and hope to die," I said.

"Deal," he answered. "And now, let's get your wool and start you on your way before this snow gets worse."

I made my goodbyes to Anne, thanked her for her gracious hospitality and made my way to the front door to change shoes.

"See you in the spring, Jenny," she called after us. "And, please, keep the slippers."

Inside the warehouse, my pulse went into overdrive. Huge cartons, stacks of shelves, and large wooden barrels overflowed with every conceivable colour of wool. I gave a whoosh of delight and ran my hand over and over the skeins, walking the length of the building, inhaling the whole thing. Two huge tables in the centre of the building were piled with sweaters in all sizes and colours and weights. Some were cardigans, some turtlenecks, all were patterned. I couldn't get enough of it. Robert pushed a pile of sweaters aside and sat on the edge of a table. He didn't say a word, just watched. I knew he understood.

I finally came to rest beside him, still keeping a hand on one of the sweaters and wanting, with all that was in me, to throw myself on top of them.

"Surely Anne didn't knit all these?" I asked. "There've got to be dozens of garments here."

"We both did some," he said. "The others are done by local women around the county."

"At last," I said, "a man who knits and doesn't think it's silly."

"Of course I knit." He looked down at his chest. "I knitted this one. It's very therapeutic and, given my situation, it'd be silly not to, don't you think?" He stood up. "Now let's see your knitting, and we'll find the proper colour for you."

I dumped out my stuff, and within very few minutes, he'd gone straight to a carton, returning with the exact shade of green I needed for Helen's present.

"Here you go," he said. "These three skeins will be enough to finish. That's going to be a handsome sweater. Your friend will love it, I'm sure."

"What's that huge pile of stuff over by the door?" I pointed to plastic covered bales of what looked like raw fleece, sitting beside the entrance. "Is it waiting to be spun into yarn?"

"Come and I'll show you." We walked to the door, and he reached into a hole in some plastic covering, pulling out a handful of fleece. "It's poor grade wool." He carefully separated a couple of strands, and straightening one out, broke off a piece about two inches long. "Look, see how it's fat at the top and bottom and thin in the middle?" I peered at it closely. He was right. It had an hourglass shape to it.

"The thin part is where the sheep was sick. It's pretty obvious once you know about it. This shipment is sub-standard. It'll never make good yarn."

"What was wrong with your sheep?"

"Oh, it's not from my sheep. I buy fleece from sheep farmers all over this part of the country who don't want to get involved in the whole yarn process. They ship it here, as you see it, and I take it from there." He stuck the ball of fleece back in the bale. "This lot, of course, won't be bought for yarn. I only deal with good quality wool."

"Then what'll happen to it? You send it back?"

"No," he said, "it'll be used for felt. When a sheep is sheared, only the fleece from the back and chest is used for yarn. The legs and underbelly shearings are turned into hats and other felt products."

"Boy," I said, "I'm certainly getting an education today. This is fascinating." I looked out the door. Thick flakes were blowing and swirling up a miniature maelstrom around the yard. "But I'd better get going. Things are not looking up."

"It's been a pleasure meeting you, Jenny, and happy knitting. Remember, when you've finished your current project, we also ship by courier, so call us any time. Be happy to send you anything you need."

"My next project is a full-length Aran coat, and that shade of bone over there would be perfect."

"You want to take it now?"

"I'd better not, or I'll be tempted to start it immediately. I've already lost a week on Helen's, and I've got dog coats to knit."

He raised an eyebrow at that, but like before, didn't comment.

"Well, I'm off now for sure, albeit reluctantly, and thanks again, Robert. I've thoroughly enjoyed today." He walked over to the car with me, carrying my package of wool. I climbed in and rolled down the window to shake his hand. "Please say goodbye and my thanks to Anne. By the way, how come she's feeding that lamb? Did its mother die?"

"She rejected it. Ewes do that sometimes, you know. Like a number of other animal species. So Anne takes over. She loves doing it, says it's just like having her own babies all over again without quite so much work. Trouble is, most of the lambs that get rejected have something wrong with them and nearly always die at an early age. She finds that hard to handle." He brushed the snow off his beard. "It's actually an interesting phenomenon. It's as if the mother knows that, and, as a result, deliberately refuses to suckle them."

"Really?" I was amazed.

"They're not always right, but it happens enough times to make it noticeable." He shrugged. "Every now and again, a couple of them do very well, and that's enough to keep Anne going. Where there's life, there's hope, I guess."

"Anyway," he slapped the car roof a couple of times and stepped back, "you'd better get going. Drive safely."

•

The snow was much thicker now, driving down with a fury, and it took me four times as long to get back to my collector lane for the highway. A snail's pace was the safest way to take the road conditions, but it turned out not to matter. As I neared the entrance to Pop's Place, three police cars formed a road block across the highway. A snowplow stood off to one side closing the collector lane, and all the vehicles had lights flashing and twirling. A huddle of men in heavy winter clothing stood beside them.

A giant, made larger still by his sheepskin winter jacket, broke away from the group and waved me into Pop's driveway. He walked up to the car window and leaned over.

"Sorry, ma'am. You'll have to pull off. We're closing the road."

"But I've got to get home." I pointed across the road. "I was just about to get onto the highway."

"No can do. Highway's closed too. Transport trailer's overturned across the road, a coupla miles down. This is as far as you go."

Did he have to sound so bloody smug about it?

"How long do you expect it to be closed?" I asked him.

"Could be an allnighter." He looked up and then at his watch. "Light's goin' already, and it's not even four yet."

"Isn't there another route I can take?"

"Ma'am," he spoke very slowly this time, one clipped word after the next, "look around you. See anything? All the county and access roads are closed. I expect they'll be open by morning, when the plows are finished." He stepped back a bit and grinned. "That is, if this little blow doesn't turn into a blizzard."

He reminded me of the weatherman on our local television channel. Couldn't stop smiling when he had really bad weather to tell you about.

"Now, why don't you just pull into Pop's here and book one of his rooms for the night? Maybe be thankful I stopped you here and not a few miles further down."

He did have a point there, so I just nodded and drove on into my breakfast spot, parking outside the motel door this time. The door swung open just as I made a dash for it, and in a flash, I was inside brushing snow off and stamping my feet.

"Well, hello again," Pop smiled from behind the desk in the cramped little office. "Weather get ya?"

"Seems it did," I said, "and it also seems I'll be staying here tonight, so I'll need one of your 'best' rooms."

He turned the register towards me and made a fuss of selecting a key.

"Put you in the room right next to here," he said. "You sure don't want to be walking any further than you have to—not in that outfit anyway. Got a colour TV, spanking new mattress and everything. You'll be snug as a bug in a rug."

"Thanks, Pop." I put my credit card back in my wallet and picked up the key. "By the way, do I dial nine or anything to get a line out?"

"Rooms don't have phones. Got a phone booth by the gas pumps but, seeing as it's snowed in too, you can use this one." He pushed an old black rotary phone across the desk and nodded towards the window. "Better hurry, though. Last time Jack operated the snowplow, he drove it smack into the utility box and knocked out the phones."

"Thank you. It's long distance, so I'll reverse the charges."

He waited until he heard me tell the operator it was a collect call, then disappeared through a door at the back, saying over his shoulder, "Come on over and eat soon—in case the power goes off as well."

"God," I thought, "is this a punishment for something?"

Helen wasn't home, so the operator and I had a little dance around until she found Shirley's number and put the call through there.

"Don't ask, Shirl. I need to make this quick. Just make sure you get hold of Helen tonight sometime. Tell her I'm stuck, so give her the number here, and say I'll be home in the morning." I listened for a minute. "Everything's fine, Shirley, except I forgot my phone, and I just don't want her worrying."

Two hours later, I was propped up at the foot of the new mattress listening to static on the television set and watching wavy lines going across the screen. There were only two channels available, and the reception was the same on both. Oh, well, at least dinner had been good, the power obviously still holding.

I hadn't seen any cows around the diner on either of my two stops, so I opted for a striploin steak, well done, baked potato with sour cream and green beans with garlic and almonds. Pop might have sounded like the voice of doom earlier, but he sure cooked a mean dinner. There was only the two of us in the restaurant. Pop's wife was "down to her sister's", and they apparently didn't get tourists at this time of year, "mostly salesmen and deer hunters."

He waited until I finished eating then brought a cup of

coffee over, sat down and quizzed me about my visit to the Delurey's. It was obvious he was dying to know what I was doing in this neck of the woods in the middle of a snowstorm, and seeing as he'd been decent enough to me, I told him the story of Cathy, the shootings and the missing green colour. His jaw dropped on the first line of my tale and stayed there until the end. Probably gave him enough ammunition to hold his own in conversation for the whole winter.

I brought a piece of homemade apple pie and a carton of milk back to the room with me for insurance. Who knew what else would happen in God's country between now and tomorrow morning?

I clicked off the television and wandered around. The room was pretty basic but spotlessly clean. So clean there wasn't even an old magazine to read. A radio was bolted to the dresser, but it was even more staticky than the television. Another glance out the window showed the same scene as it had five minutes ago—white and no sign of changing anytime soon. I pulled the curtains shut, rechecked the door lock and went to bed with the Gideon bible.

Twenty-Three

A naked Robert Delurey stood in the shallow grave. It was newly dug in a perfect circle. When he opened his mouth to sing, it was the clear, Welsh baritone of Tom Jones that pealed out. Just one line, over and over—"I just couldn't take any more." Anne Delurey sat on the ground outside the ring of moist earth. She was laughing delightedly, head thrown back, as she watched her husband. The lamb was still cradled in her arms, but now blood flowed from a jagged gash in the little throat. The bright red thickness spilled over her wrists, onto her lap, and formed itself into a flower pattern on her ice-white skirt.

Repulsed, I turned to go, but my feet wouldn't move. I looked down. My bare feet were criss-crossed by strands of wool woven into the grass, and as I watched, their heads turned as one and two pairs of bright, knowing eyes looked straight at me, beckoning me forward.

Anne held out a crimson hand… "Come, Jenny," she said. "Come. Taste the magic." I screamed and woke up just as the arm lengthened and the fingers snaked out to grasp my arm.

With sudden, terrible clarity, I knew our killer's identity.

"Sweet Jesus," I sat up in the bed, sobbing out loud and pounded on my legs. "No. Don't let it be."

But it was, and I knew it was.

Eulah had told me the truth when she said she'd killed her

son. I just hadn't seen it, had thought she was only speaking figuratively. Killed him by her inadequacy as a mother, as outlined over the years by her loving husband. But that wasn't it at all.

Shivering and still crying, I got out of bed, dragged off the quilt and wrapped myself in it. A quick look out the window showed thick flakes still coming down. Beyond the parking lot lights, it was pitch black. My watch showed just after six, too early to rouse Pop for the phone, too early to get the Chevy gassed up, too fucking early to do anything.

I walked back and forth around the room, talking to myself, trying to stop the shivering, trying to get a grip.

"Stop and think about this, Jenny. Even if it wasn't six in the morning, even if you weren't snowed in, and even if you could gas up and head for home, what're you gonna do anyway? Charge in and save the day? Have Hobart and Bartolo cart her off?"

"But Dan Haggerty…Gerry Menard and Cathy…" I answered.

"…are dead and buried and it won't do Romeo any harm to stay in jail another day. 'Bastard', I think you called him. Besides, you don't even know for sure she killed them."

"I know. I do know. 'Cause of the sheep…think about the Delurey's sheep. They deliberately let their young die. When they know there's something wrong about them, something that stops them from growing right." I threw off the quilt and started to get dressed. "Just like she knew."

Another look out the window showed a few streaks of gray breaking the sky. The snow had stopped, and I could see black road surface across from the parking lot, and last night's roadblock was nowhere to be seen. The office and gas island lights clicked on, along with the vacancy sign. That was all I needed to clump next door.

"Pop, I need the phone. Quick."

He was behind the counter, straightening the tourist brochures I'd shuffled through last night.

"No phone. Lines are down."

"Then I need gas."

"Now?"

"Right now. Please, Pop."

I was on the highway by a quarter to seven. Large snowbanks, deposited by the plows, loomed alongside, but the road was pretty clear, though the going was agonizingly slow. Not for the first time, I was grateful for the Chevy's bulk and the way it motored solidly along. A box lid was on the seat beside me, holding the pie and carton of milk from last night. Eulah Jones sat on the other side of the box.

Pop had promised to keep trying the phone. "What d'you want me to say if your friend answers?"

"Just tell her I'm on my way, and that George is right. She'll understand."

The radio told me the weather front had passed, travelling east, and that road conditions had "improved". I passed quite a number of cars off to the side, some at crazy angles and mentally apologized to the cop who'd waved me over last night. I might be crawling, but at least I was mobile.

Rounding a corner about forty miles down the highway, I spotted a gas station off to the left and hooked a turn into the entrance, skidded and slid sideways along a snowbank. The car gave a huge hiccup but didn't cut out. Well now, I thought, isn't this just bloody lovely, and started to crank down the window but stopped when I got a face full of snow. I tried backing up, but the wheels dug in and started spinning. I knew enough about the old car to stop at that point. The weight would've simply dug me in deeper, and since I couldn't open the door against the wall of snow, the only thing left to do was blow the horn and hopefully raise somebody from the adjacent house or garage. I kept up the staccato blasts for a full five minutes before a figure materialized from behind the mountain of snow and came over to the passenger side. I scooted across the seat and rolled down the window.

"Help you?" A woman's voice, though you wouldn't have guessed it from looking at her. The only thing visible under the huge parka hood was the top half of a round, red face and two scrunched up eyes half-hidden by two caterpillar eyebrows.

"I'm stuck," I said.

"See that," came the reply. Christ, was she related to Tiny?

"Can you get me out? It's an emergency. I have to report a murder."

The eyebrows disappeared up into the hood. "Stay in the car. Be right back."

She beetled off towards the house before I could move the box off the seat onto the floor and get out the passenger door. My sneakers sank up to the laces in the snow, so I just stood where I was and waited. My frustration level was off the scale by now.

No more than three minutes later, I swung around at the sound of barking and saw double. There were two of them now, in matching parkas, coming at me—only this time one of them was holding a leash attached to a huge German shepherd.

"Murder?" A man this time. "Whose murder?"

I opened the car door and plonked backwards down on the seat, facing them, thinking Welcome to God's Country. Oh, fuck it, I muttered. By this time, I was too drained to be scared—either by him or his dog.

He repeated his question.

"Look, just let me explain, then you'll see why I need you to get me out of here fast, or at least let me use your phone."

"Phone's down. Start talking." The man again.

I got it all out, non-stop, in twenty minutes or so. "So you can see why I have to get to a phone."

They looked at each other, turned around and walked away a few steps for a confab. I heard the name Delurey a couple of times, then he nodded and she shrugged in some unspoken agreement—the first positive thing I'd seen since I'd left Pop's place. She handed the dog's leash to her husband and walked away without a word, but then I wasn't looking to make friends with either of them. I just wanted back on the road.

"Wait here," my benefactor growled. "The truck'll pull you out, and then you'd best be gone."

It took some doing, but after three-quarters of an hour of hooking chains to the Chevy's bumper and a lot of gear meshing, dog snarling and metal groaning, I was ready for the road.

"I can't thank you enough." I reached across the seat for my purse and looked at him through the open window. "What do I owe you?"

"Nothing."

"But…"

"Just be on your way."

"Hold on." I hadn't even seen her come back. "Take this." She handed me a black plastic car mug. "Hot coffee." Another shrug. "Sometimes you gotta do what you gotta do."

I managed to get a "thank you both" out and drove away before the tears started again.

I put the idea of finding a phone out of my mind and decided to head straight for home. I'd had enough of country life to last a lifetime.

It took me nearly four hours to negotiate the hundred-odd kilometres of deserted road. Hours of utter frustration and nearly going demented wondering what to do with my awful knowledge.

I knew, of course, what that was. But I also knew—when I finally pulled into our driveway with a silent word of thanks—after arguing with myself for the whole drive, that if Gerry Menard and Cathy Haggerty hadn't been innocent victims in this tragedy, I wouldn't have done a thing.

The woman had suffered so much over the years and without a doubt was suffering still. I looked over at her, still dressed in mourning black, and saw her torment. Would locking her up serve any real purpose? Wasn't she already finished with hope?

"At least allow her to bury her son," I said. "At least that. Then decide."

"Jenny," my mother said from the back seat, "you know what's right. Do it."

•

Eb and Neb charged me as I opened the back door and, without stopping to take off my shoes, headed for the phone. Helen's voice came through from the front hall.

"I'm in here," she said.

I dropped the phone back in the cradle and crossed through the kitchen. She sat on the floor, back against the wall and facing the cupboard door, knees drawn up to her chest and her chin resting on folded arms. Her jet black hair fell in front of her face, hiding it. The pups, right behind me, put on the brakes a few feet from the "cold spot" and began barking furiously.

"Shut up," I yelled. "No more animal insight. Not today."

They ignored me. I looked down at Helen and took a deep breath. "Eulah Jones…" I said, over the noise.

"…is dead." she looked up. Her eyes looked like two raw welts.

"Oh, Christ," I slid down the wall and sat facing her.

"Christ had nothing to do with it," Helen said. "She shot herself…" a hoarse sound as she cleared her throat, "…and I helped her."

•

Eulah had arrived on our doorstep on Sunday morning around eleven, just about the same time I was watching Anne Delurey feed the lamb. She'd looked so distraught at finding me gone for the day that Helen had asked her in for coffee.

"She was exactly as you described, Jenny, when you met her on Saturday. A lost soul. My heart went out to her." Her mouth formed a wry smile. "Little did I know."

She stood up.

"Let's go into the kitchen. I need a drink before I tell you the rest."

I set the dogs outside and put a match to the fire, while she half-filled two glasses with whisky and ran them quickly past the cold water tap, making sure not a lot fell in. We sat down and Helen picked up her recitation.

"She fidgeted the whole time, couldn't sit still. Hands fluttering like a bird and eyes darting around the room. Kept saying she needed to talk to you. Something about her daughter and your mother. I'd heard the weather reports and told her you'd probably be quite late. Could I help her?"

The little laugh came again and she downed some more whisky.

"Well, I helped her, all right. I took the letter she'd brought for you, stuck it up on the mantle and showed her to the front door."

I looked up. The mantle was bare.

"Where's the letter?"

"When Shirley called and said you wouldn't be home, I read it, late last night. I thought it might have something to do with the funeral this morning."

"And…?"

"I read it. And then I burned it."

I topped up our glasses from the bottle on the floor beside us.

"Helen, I can see you're terribly upset, and I can only imagine what you've been through, but so help me Christ, if you don't spit all of it out immediately, I'll knock you flat."

"It was a confession. A confession just like its author, stark and pathetic. She apologized for Menard and Cathy. They weren't meant to die, just Stephen. But she'd never used a gun before. Said she looked at her husband and saw her son. Looked in the mirror and saw the future melt into the past."

She drained her glass and stared at the fire.

"I read it to the end. Neglect, abuse, the sins of the father, etc., all of it. Not detailed, of course, that wasn't her way, but clear as a bell nevertheless and quite dispassionately written."

"Was it revenge, Helen? Killing his pride and joy? Was that it?"

"No," she shook her head. "There was no hate, no altruistic motive, no Hollywood script—nothing that dramatic. I could've handled any of those."

Her short laugh held a touch of hysteria this time. "The last line in the letter was 'I've had enough.'"

I looked at her, eyebrows raised. She nodded.

"It was that simple. Three lives wasted, or four now, I guess, because one sad, little, ninety-pound woman just simply had had enough."

She closed her eyes and sat back in the chair. But it wasn't finished yet.

"Helen, the rest. Out with it. Let's get this done with."

"Okay, here's the rest. She went to the funeral this morning, handed an envelope to her husband, went into the antechamber and shot herself in the head. Same gun." She gave a harsh laugh. "No wonder the cops didn't find it. We'll never even know where she got it."

She leaned forward and picked up the bottle. I snatched it out of her hand.

"You couldn't have known, Helen. Don't do this."

"Of course I knew. Why do you think I burned the letter?"

Twenty-Four

Saturday, November 14, 9:30 a.m.

Gathered and ready, we stood outside the mall entrance doors—Santa in his tractor-driven sleigh, a group of assorted-sized elves in little red suits with white fur trim, the police pipe band, splendid in their kilts, and a full corps of drum majorettes complete with fire batons.

I nodded to the Drum Major.

"Let's go."

Jessica Burton was born in Scotland. Her father joined BOAC (the British airline), and the family moved around the world for the next six years.

She emigrated to Canada in the 50s and completed schooling in Toronto. Jessica spent seven years with the *Brampton Guardian* newspaper and also worked for many years in the shopping centre industry. All of these experiences have aided in the formation of the unique insider's take on the workings of the shopping mall and newspaper industries contained in *Death Goes Shopping*, her first novel and first work with RendezVous Press.

A single mother of four grown children, she lives in Brampton, Ontario. She is currently working on the next Jenny Turnbull novel.